The Race Is On!

Melisa Calcote

The Race Is On!
Copyright © 2024 by Melisa Calcote. All rights reserved.

No part of this publication may be reproduced, stored in a retrieval system or transmitted in any way by any means, electronic, mechanical, photocopy, recording or otherwise without the prior permission of the author except as provided by USA copyright law.

The opinions expressed by the author are not necessarily those of URLink Print and Media.

1603 Capitol Ave., Suite 310 Cheyenne, Wyoming USA 82001
1-888-980-6523 | admin@urlinkpublishing.com

URLink Print and Media is committed to excellence in the publishing industry.

Book design copyright © 2024 by URLink Print and Media. All rights reserved.

Published in the United States of America

Library of Congress Control Number: 2024910186
ISBN 978-1-68486-784-4 (Paperback)
ISBN 978-1-68486-787-5 (Hardback)
ISBN 978-1-68486-786-8 (Digital)

15.05.24

Chapter 1: The Wooers that Dance 1

Chapter 2: Tim Spent Time
with his Brother and Wife 6

Chapter 3: The Artist's Favourite Portrait 11

Chapter 4: Tim Paints his Brother's Wife 13

Chapter 5: Tim's Enjoyable Relaxation Indoors 16

Chapter 6: The Portrait (The Sitting) 18

Chapter 7: The Discussion 21

Chapter 8: The Garden Picture of Katrina 24

Chapter 9: The Picture of a Field (A Model's Pose) 26

Chapter 10: Tim's Last Personal Delivery 29

Chapter 11: The Sitting 31

Chapter 12: The Artist's Triumph 34

Chapter 13: The Artist's Last Moment
(With the Company of a Model) 38

Chapter 14: The Request for Painting 43

Chapter 15: The Artist's Last Resort to Paint 46

Chapter 16: The Artist's Times Alone with Nature 49

CHARACTERS

Jenny Smythe Brooks, about 33 years old, now married to David Brooks for three years. Jenny is now working at the Community Medical Center three to four days a week as a nurse, as it was what she had majored in college. She wanted to continue in this field as well as help Rosa, their housemaid around the house whenever she was needed.

David Brooks, about the same age as Jenny, found work on the island an Architect Engineer for his abilities for architect design for those other businesses that were growing up around on the island.

Jeremy Smyth, He was about 39 years old. Although Jeremy was raised by Aunt Jessie's sister, Julia George; he chose his last name to Smythe as was agreed upon between his adopted mom and his real mom, Jill Smythe.

Jill and Roger Smythe – they came to stay with Jenny and David for a few weeks. It turned into a couple of months as during their stay, something comes up with Jenny and Jeremy that causes them to stay a little longer. Jill had her own business that she was able to put on hold until she and her husband returned to the states where they lived. Roger had already narrowed his career down to a slower pace as he was a Landscape Designer, which helped Jeremy out quite a bit with what he enjoyed doing around the grounds of the villa.

Charlie Gordon, the youngest son of Mrs. Jessie Gordon, who agreed to stay at the villa with his cousins, Jenny, and Jeremy. He wanted to stay in his own room for now, and continue to work with the horses he had raised there on the Gordon Villa.

Rosa, the housemaid. Rosa started working for the Gordon family almost 30 years ago, for Mrs. Jessie. She started working at the villa during a hard time after her own mother had passed away when she was a teenager. Mrs. Jessie took her in and gave her a place to live and a steady job. Rosa had pretty much been there during the whole time when Charlie was growing up. She was already considered a part of the family and enjoyed cooking in the kitchen with Mrs. Jessie; and now with Jenny, who also had the same desire as her aunt. Rosa came to discover that Jenny was more like Mrs. Jessie in so many ways.

Mrs. Doris and Reverend Harold Barclay, Head of 'New Horizons': a one floor organization that was , developed by Mrs. Jessie Gordon three years before she passed away. It was her way of giving back to the community that she was a big part for so many years. She brought on Mrs. Doris and Reverend Harold Barclay to be over the organization and had also left a certain percentage of her assets that was in her will, to help keep it running until such time that Charlie and Jenny chose to continue contributing to it also.

Joseph McEnroe and daughter, Caroline, owner/rider of a Race horse called 'Firecracker.'

Fireball– 3 years old, son of Chantilly and Ghost Rider; who is son of Tornado.

THE RACE IS ON!

It was the beginning of spring of the third year that Jenny Smythe and David Brooks had been married. It was this year that would change their lives completely and everything around them. This family continues to thrive together within the Gordon Villa, as they encounter new challenges in their lives as well as the anticipation of things to come or the unexpected visitors that come into their lives.

Charlie Gordon and his cousin, Jeremy Smyth, were at the horse races in Barbados. The fans were coming in, making their bets, and finding themselves a good place to sit. Charlie was in the stall with Fireball and Jeremy stood on the outside looking in as he was brushing him down.

"Come on in Jeremy. I'm sure I could use your help in here. He needs his nutrition, you know," Jeremy slowly opened the gate; he inched around Fireball as he faced him.

"Good boy," Jeremy said patting his neck, "It is okay. Uncle Jeremy's not going to hurt you." Charlie laughed at him because Fireball would always do something crazy to throw Jeremy off guard.

"Come on, you are still skittish around him? How long is it going to take for you to get used to him? He has already gotten used to you."

"I know. That's what bothers me. I never know what he is going to do next," Jeremy said as he pulls out some carrots to feed him. Fireball took a chunk out of one of the carrots and was chewing on it while he was watching Jeremy.

"Don't give me that look. You know exactly what I am talking about," then he fed him the rest of the carrot, "You win this race, Uncle Jeremy will give you a whole bunch of carrots. By George, where in the world is that jockey?" he said looking around.

"Do not worry, Jeremy. He will be here. It is only twenty minutes till the race begins." At the front gate was Alex Rodriquez, a local, who loved horses and had been riding since he was a teenager. This was to be his job of the season and was hoping he would be able to stick with Fireball, for he had already seen what the horse could do. He was there when he saw Charlie riding him to help him get used to racing and pick up his speed through several different obstacles. As he made his way through the crowd, he thought to himself how he could encourage Fireball to go faster than the other horses.

"Boy, he's got character too," he said out loud to himself, "This is going to be interesting." He made it to the line of horse stalls as he started looking for Charlie and stall number 14.

"Can't be that hard to find," he thought to himself, "However he has got a goof of a cousin. I wonder what side of the family he came from."

Then he spotted them in the stall with Fireball.

"Hey man. How's it going?" Alex asked when he walked over to them.

"Pretty good," Charlie said he was sponging him down with a cool sponge. "I am glad you made it. You're going to really enjoy this. Fireball's ready for you."

Alex stroked his nose as Fireball nudged his hand. "Hey boy. Are you ready for this?"

Fireball nodded like he understood every word. They opened the gate to let Alex in. He came in and patted him on his back. He had already done the warm up laps with him earlier in the day. As he climbed up on Fireball, Jeremy immediately moved out of his way.

"You're not used to him?" Alex asked him.

"Not quite. But I am getting there. I'm telling you. This horse is unpredictable. You never know what he is going to do next," Jeremy said backing up to let them out. Fireball looked around at him.

"Yeah, I'm talking about you. Don't give me that look. There you go again." Alex smiled at Jeremy, as he realized that he liked that in a horse.

"That's what I like about him," Alex said as he was walking him around.

Aunt Jessie's villa consisted of seven bedrooms, kitchen, dining room, recreation room and what they liked to call the family room. She owned ten acres as the barn and stables were located to the back right side of the property. There was a gate that led to the back yard and the patio door from the family room that led out onto the patio in the rear of the house. The grounds were immaculately kept up by Jeremy, who always enjoyed doing the yard work and keeping the rose garden beautifully designed. Jenny usually would help Rosa in keeping the house cleaned when she was not working as a nurse at the local clinic not far from the house; and would often help prepare and cook the meals. At the back part of the yard, there was the swing that sat under a big tree that pointed in the direction of the meadow behind the house, and the beach just beyond the forest. It was the best place to sit and watch the sunrise. By this time, Charlie had two new horses he had started working with also. One was four years old that he called 'Ole Henry.' The other one was close to five years and his name was 'Jackson.' Both horses were born from a line of pure thoroughbreds. It was Charlie's passion to work with horses and make them good show horses or race horses. He had plans to get these two ready for show horses as he also started making progress to prepare Fireball for the races. He knew Fireball was going to be quite a character being that he was also unpredictable. And he also knew that it would be a riot to watch Jeremy as Fireball became to be more like him. But Jeremy did not know was that he would one day find out that Fireball will be his horse.

Meanwhile, in Bridgetown, Jenny was in the family room sitting in the rocker putting her shoes on.

"Come on David. We are going to be late if you don't get on the ball." Then she heard him coming down the stairs and she got up to meet him at the bottom of the staircase.

"I'm ready dear," he said.

"I'm excited. This is Fireball's first race," Jenny said before getting into the jeep.

"Yea, I know. How is it you were ready before me?" David asked slipping in behind the wheel.

"It doesn't take me any time when I'm in a hurry to be somewhere. You should know that by now," she smiled then leaned over and kissed him. Then they were on their way.

It was ten till the hour, Roger came back to his seat beside Jill, with a couple of drinks in his hands.

"Here you go dear," he said before sitting down. "I know she said they'll be here soon."

"Don't worry. They will."

He scanned the crowd down below to see if he could see them yet, and then he spotted them and waved to them. They came up the steps to where they were sitting.

"Thanks dad. David was running late this time," she said sitting down beside him and David sat on the other side.

The jockeys were leading their horses into the starting gates and getting into their positions. Alex was with Fireball in the gate talking to him.

"Okay boy. Do you remember what this is like?" he asked as he noticed Fireball nodding; and was a little astonished, "Alright then. Let's do this. Just remember, you want to get as far ahead of the other horses as possible. Okay?" It was then when he realized why he was named Fireball for he was getting restless and fired up.

Just as the gates buzzed open with a loud bell sound, the horses were off into a speed of lightning that left a cloud of dust behind. Fireball picked up speed when he got halfway through the course, when he came up beside a filly called Firecracker. Who would have thought that he would be racing against a beauty like her? They were running side by side when Fireball eyeballed the light-colored filly beside him. When Alex tried to get him to pass her up, Fireball tended to hold back and run right beside her as both them were in the lead side by side.

"Come on boy. You can flirt later," Alex whispered in his ear. At first Fireball hesitated as he was momentarily side tracked and had one thing on his mind. They could hear the announcers over the crowd as everyone in the stands were urging one or the other on.

"And it is Fireball and Firecracker neck in neck for the lead. What a pair. Looks like they seem to have a team effort going on here," he shouted over the loud speakers. When Fireball realized she was in this for the win, his instincts kicked in, and he began moving his way ahead as fast as he could to pass her up. Jenny and the others were shouting "Come on boy. You can do it."

"Atta boy," Alex said as Fireball was speeding up. But before he realized it, so was Firecracker and then the home stretch seemed much longer as time seemed to slow down. It was at the quarter of a mile when Firecracker starting passing him up from behind and she won by a nose ahead of Fireball. But he came in second, which was still good for Fireball.

Everyone was excited that Firecracker won the race since Fireball was a little new at this. Alex was about to ride around toward the stalls as people were taking pictures of Firecracker and the rider, Hank. Even the press got a picture of Alex riding Fireball for the paper. A reporter started asking Alex questions.

"Who's the owner of this fine-looking horse?"

"That would be Charlie Gordon," Alex said as he noticed Charlie and Jeremy walking up.

The reporter, Ben, turned around when he noticed that Alex was waving toward Charlie. "How are you doing today?"

"Okay, I guess, given its' his first race. I think he did pretty good," Charlie said coming up beside Fireball and patted his neck.

"Yea, that was a close race there. Wasn't it? Looks like he has got competition with the filly Firecracker. Do you think he will pass her up next time?"

"Probably will. That is, if he remembers what he is out here to do," Jeremy said.

"We will see how that goes. He is going to have some tough training in these next few weeks," Charlie said as the reporter took a picture of them. Fireball looked around at him. Jeremy was tempted to say something, but bit his lip instead. Then Alex got off, and they started walking back toward the stall.

After they turned the corner to go down the row of stalls, people were coming and going. Jenny, David, and her parents came up beside them.

"He did good," Jenny said when she pulled out an apple from her bag and gave it to Fireball, which he was grateful to get since the guys were quiet.

"Yea Fireball got beat by a filly. How awkward is that?" Jeremy asked.

"Hey wait a minute. That filly has been racing for the last two years," she said shaking her finger at him. "And after all, Fireball did come in at second place."

"That's true," Charlie said, "He's just got to learn not mix business with pleasure." Alex had a time holding on to him as he was shaking his head.

"It's okay Fireball," he said stroking his neck, "You still get the carrots," Alex said looking at the others and gave them the 'quiet' sign. Not long after getting Fireball back home into his own stall, they all met in the family room along with Alex.

"Okay. What is the plan now?" David asked Charlie.

"He has got a few small races coming up, so we need to get him ready for those.

"And what if this pretty little filly shows up too?" Jeremy asked leaning on the mantle.

"Well, I've got an idea we need to check into," Alex spoke up clearing his throat.

"Oh really Dr. Alex? And what would you suggest?"

"Well, most times when you bring the two horses together; you let them get to know each other first. And then make them run a one-on-one race. Nine times out of ten, they will get the picture."

"And if we don't do that?" Charlie asked.

"Fireball will most likely let her win every race she's in with him."

"That makes sense," Charlie said and the others agreed.

A spirit had appeared there beside Jeremy listening in on the conversation. The spirit was so close by Jeremy that it made him shiver, and he was shaking his arms and rubbing them.

"Are you okay Jeremy?" David asked when he noticed his reaction.

"I just got chill all of a sudden," he said stepping away from the mantle.

"Are you cold?"

"No man. I'm okay."

In another part of the room, Michael faded in to see what was going on. He noticed the spirit of a short man standing by the mantle where Jeremy once stood. Although he was a man of short stature, he had the physique of a strong able body. Then Michael knew he had to research this to see who in the family this might be, so he faded back out. Jeremy had walked over to the chair where his sister was sitting and leaned on the arm of the chair.

"If you don't have plans, you can join us." Charlie said to Alex

"We need to contact Firecrackers' owner and see if we could arrange a time for them to meet," Alex said.

"I saw that name on the schedule," Jenny said as she pulled it out of her shirt pocket. "That would be Joseph McEnroe. Is he from the island?" she asked Charlie.

"Yes, I know of that family," he said when he picked up the telephone book that was laying on the end table. Once he found his number, Charlie called him on his cell phone. Everyone was quiet as he talked to someone on the other end. Charlie wrote down information on a tablet and then said 'Thank you' and hung up.

"Good news," he said. "We can bring Fireball over there in the morning to meet Firecracker."

"That's good," Jeremy said, "What if this plan backfires on us?" he asked Alex.

"Not to worry. If that happens, we go to plan B." Jeremy was afraid to ask what plan B was, so he didn't. About that time, Rosa, the housemaid, came into the room and announced that dinner was ready. Rosa had been with the Gordon family since she was a teenager, when Mrs. Jessie had taken her in after her mom had passed away. Mrs. Jessie Gordon gave her a place to live and work also. Rosa was now in her forties.

"If you don't have plans, you could join us," Charlie said to Alex.

"No, not really," he said stuffing the kays back into his pocket. He followed Charlie into the dining room where Rosa already had dishes of food set in the middle of the table. The spirit had followed them into the dining room and stood at a distance away from the table. The dinner conversation was mostly about the agenda for the next few days.

After dinner, Jeremy, Charlie, and Alex walked out to check on Fireball. Jeremy opened the gate and went inside the stall to retrieve a bag of carrots back in the corner. The he realized that Fireball had completely turned around and was facing him, for he knew that familiar smell

"No, you can't have all of these at the same time," Jeremy said and he was attempting to get by the hungry horse.

"Come on boy, let him out, Fireball," Charlie said coaxing him to turn back around. Fireball looked at Jeremy and gave a snort before turning around.

"I know," Jeremy said as he was able to retreat to the other side of the gate, "You thought you were really going to get me this time." Fireball snorted at him again and got him good with nose fluid.

"Mind your manners," Charlie said to him as Jeremy had dropped the carrots on the ground to clean himself off with a towel that was hanging close by. As soon as he picked up some of the carrots, Jeremy looked at Fireball.

"You know, I really shouldn't give these to you at all since you're acting like this," Charlie sort of smiled at him.

"But you wouldn't do that," Charlie said.

"Oh really? Why not?"

"Yeah, he reminds you too much of yourself. You know, the way you used to be like."

Jeremy heard Alex snicker behind him and turned around.

"Very funny."

"So, I guess they pick at each other like this all the time?" Alex asked.

"Yea, you can say that. They know what they can get away with."

Humm," Jeremy said and Fireball let them know he heard that too with a snort.

Jeremy started to feed him the carrots. "You don't let that get to you boy," he said rubbing his neck. After the sixth carrot, Charlie said "Hey, he doesn't need too much fattening up," he said walking over to Fireball.

The Race Is On!

"So boy, do you want to go meet this Firecracker?" As soon as he got the words out, Fireball let out a neigh as if he were saying "Yes!" Charlie rubbed his nose. "You'll get to meet her tomorrow." Fireball had his tail held high as if he was saying "I am excited."

"You see," Alex said, "He definitely wants to meet her outside of the social life of racing."

"Alright," Jeremy said, "Let's hope this works."

"Man, you worry too much."

"That's because he's got money betting on Fireball to win the next big race," Charlie said.

"Whoa. I guess I would be worried also. I am just the jockey."

The following morning came with a beautiful sunrise as David and Jenny were walking through the flower garden back behind the house.

"You were restless last night," David said, "Are you okay?"

"Yea, I think something I ate that didn't agree with me. I woke up earlier this morning throwing up."

"Uh oh. I hope you aren't coming down with something," he said as he had his arm around her.

"I will be okay dear. I want to go with them to see Firecracker too. She is a pretty horse."

"Yea, she is. It'll be funny if we cannot tear them apart when we leave." Jenny smiled at that.

The spirit that appeared inside the night before faded into view not far from Fireball's stable. It kind of startled the horse as he let out a small neigh, and you could see the whites of his eyes. "You startled me!" Fireball said suddenly.

"It's okay boy. You can trust me. You can talk?" he asked alarmed.

"Not just for anyone. Who are you?"

"So, you're the son of Ghost Rider," he said rubbing his nose lightly.

"Yeah, that's me."

"Did you know Ghost Rider is the son of Tornado?"

Fireball shook his head. "No, I didn't know that far back," he said as his ears perked up in curiosity.

"I hear you're going to meet a pretty young filly," he said. "Yea, I know all about that. Whatever you do, you don't mix business with pleasure, if you know what I mean."

"Well, that is going to be hard to do, since she is such a pretty sight to see. Why?"

"Well, that's what happened to Tornado. And it took me the longest time to get his head back in the game of racing," he said looking up at him. "You are from a long line of racing, my boy. Don't you forget that. That there is your heritage." Then the man stepped back as he heard footsteps coming. "I will be talking to you again. Don't forget," he said as he faded out of view.

Charlie and Jeremy came walking in as David was backing up the horse trailer to the open door.

"Alright Fireball, let's go visiting," Charlie said as at first Fireball did not budge, and then gradually came out of his stall and followed his buddy into the trailer.

Before their arrival at the McEnroe's, Joseph McEnroe was out in the corral with Firecracker exercising the horse as he led her around in circles. His daughter, Caroline, walked over to the fence to watch.

"That horse Fireball coming this morning?" she asked leaning on the fence.

"Yes, I just want to get her exercise in before they get here," he said as he noticed that her head went up in excitement. "We don't know exactly how this is going to fan out, since she did beat him in the race yesterday."

Firecracker was swooshing her tail, and a small neigh came out in her excitement.

"Girl, you're excited to get company?" he asked, "You should be. He is a young one."

"I would think his pride was hurt. But then, maybe something else got in the way," Caroline said. Caroline was the youngest of his five children who still lived at home. She was dead set on being the rider for her own horse, since they started the horse racing fifteen years ago. Caroline turned around when she heard their truck pulling into the yard. Everyone had gotten out, and as Charlie opened the trailer to bring Fireball out, the others came over to say 'Hi' to them.

"Morning," Joseph said, "How are you doing?"

"Doing good," David said as they gathered around, "That is a fine horse you got there. How old is she?"

"She's five years old," Caroline said, "She gets her exercising in at least four times a day. And how old is Fireball?"

"He's three years old," David said. Charlie came walking up with Fireball with Jeremy trailing behind them. Firecracker stopped going in circles once she noticed Fireball and her ears went forward with an excitement in her eyes. Joseph led her to the fence.

"Caroline, open the barn door."

"Okay dad," she said as she went to open it, and Fireball went straight into the barn without any help and into the corral. Once she arrived back out, she said, "Why don't you all come in for some coffee while these two get acquainted?" Everyone agreed to that and followed them into the house. Jeremy was following Caroline when they went inside, and he followed her straight into the kitchen to help.

"What can I do?" Jeremy asked.

"Thanks. The coffee cups are in that cabinet you are in front of. I'll get the serving tray out," she said as she opened another cabinet below. He pulled out the cups needed for everyone and Caroline started pouring the coffee.

"So how long have you been on the island?"

"Prety much most of my life. I like it here. I usually like going to the islands close by. And you?" He was putting the filled cups on the tray.

"Oh well, I grew up in the states; but moved here about five years ago."

"That's nice, I assume they're your family," she said referring to the others in the living room.

"You assume right. But I am not married," he hinted around.

After setting everything on the serving tray, Jeremy brought the coffee into the living room where everyone was sitting around the coffee table and visiting.

"So how long have you been racing horses?" Charlie asked Joseph.

"We have been horse racing now for fifteen years. It was right after my wife passed away. I picked it up as a hobby to keep myself busy. Now it is something me and Caroline enjoy doing together."

After everyone fixed their coffee, Jeremy came to sit down by Caroline on the love seat.

"Have you had this kind of situation before?" Alex asked.

"Oh yes, I have. Firecracker is a beauty and since she has met other horses before, she has not bore a filly yet. But if that does happen, she will be out of racing until after birth; and I will just put in one of my other thoroughbreds."

Charlie was relieved to know this since he figured that this just might happen. Meanwhile, out in the corral, Fireball was following Firecracker around from the corral into the barn and back. When she finally stopped long enough for him to catch up with her, the spirit showed up right in front of them.

"Now kids," he said talking to them, "If you get involved here, one of you is going to have to withdraw from racing for a while. You know that. Do you really want that?"

"But I'm just getting to know this beautiful lady," Fireball said, he said looking him straight in the eye. Firecracker turned to him "You talk?"

"Yeah, But not just anyone. But for you, you got my full attention," Fireball said to her. Both the horses looked at him and looked back at each other, as Firecracker had her ears cocked back she was thinking about the situation.

"That doesn't mean we can't be friends, right?"

"Right," the spirit said. "So have fun getting to know each other. There is no harm in that. But if you take your friendship further, you know, you never know." He said shrugging his shoulders.

They agreed to that. "Hey Fireball," Firecracker said getting his attention, "Don't worry. I will let you win some races."

"Oh, I get it. If I can match your skill, maybe we got some good times together?"

"Don't you worry about that sweetie," she nodded at him, "You had me on first glance," and she neighed after that.

So, after the spirit left, they were just playing around and getting to know each other in their own language before their owners came back outside. When they approached the fence, they were running in circles around the coral.

"Hey look," Jenny said, "Looks like they're getting their exercise."

"Yea," Caroline said leaning against the fence, "You hope that's all they did." Jeremy shrugged and smiled at her. Little did he know that she was going to start being Firecrackers rider.

Fireball walked over to the side where Charlie was standing and nudged his hand up on his nose. "Did you have a good time?" Charlie asked him. Fireball nodded his head up and down.

"That's good. I guess you got a new friend now," he said rubbing his neck now. Firecracker came walking up beside Fireball and rubbed up against him with her nose with a soft neigh.

"Does that answer your question?" Jeremy asked.

"Yep, I do believe. Well, boy, are you ready to go? We have some things to do today."

Fireball turned toward Firecracker and looked her in the eyes like, 'I'll be seeing you' nod, then turned and walked through the open door of the barn.

"Okay then," Jeremy said as he walked to the other door to let him out.

Later after returning home, Jeremy went to put Fireball in his stall while the others went inside. After he got him settled, he gave him a pale of food; he started toward the house. He was almost out of the barn door when he thought he saw out of the corner of his eye the spirit had appeared in front of the stall

"Mmmm," Jeremy paused for a minute not exactly sure what he saw, "What in the world?" he whispered to himself. Then he stopped just outside the door and peeked in to see that this short man was standing there talking to Fireball.

"Huh??" He stood there for a few minutes but he could not tell what he was saying and did not want to sneak back in and startle him, so Jeremy left and went on inside. Everyone was in the family room when he came in.

"You will never guess what I just saw," They all stopped talking and looked over at Jeremy.

"Just as I was leaving from the barn, there was some kind of spirit that appeared in front of the horse stall."

"Oh?" Charlie asked, "What was it? A man or woman?"

"A short man built like you," Jeremy said.

"Me? Are you sure about that?"

"Yeah, I'm sure. He had your features."

"Ok…" he paused "I wonder who that could have been. I know there were short people on my father's side that's passed away. But I'm just not sure who it could be."

"Do you think he was built like a jockey?" Alex asked.

"It could very well be. Were there relatives that you might remember that were once jockeys?" Jeremy asked.

"I'll bet you there was," Jenny said, "There was someone that Aunt Jessie used to talk about when I was eighteen. Don't you remember Charlie?"

"Yea, I just do not remember his name. But I do know that whoever lived here before we moved here; one of my uncles, or cousins also raised horses."

"Aha!" Jeremy said, "We've got a mystery to unravel."

"Yea," Charlie said, "And find out why he is showing up now. Or Jeremy could be seeing things."

"I swear I am not just seeing things that are not there. I saw him with my own eyes."

"Was he a Gordon?" Alex asked.

"I'm pretty sure he was," Jeremy said.

"There's a library here on the island," David said, "Why don't we go there to check it out?"

"Wait a minute," Jenny said getting up to go see where her parents were. She walked out the patio door toward the flower garden. Roger and Jill were sitting on the swing under one of the big trees.

"Hey hon. How is it going? Roger asked.

"I am okay, dad. Mom, I have got a question that you might have the answer to."

"Yes dear?"

"Do you remember anyone on Uncle Joe's side that might have been a jockey?"

"Uncle Joe? Wow. That's a trick question. Because there were several of them that go way back to the 1900's."

"What? That many? I did not know it went that far back."

"Why do you ask Jen?"

"Well mom. You are not going to believe this," By the time they walked back inside with Jenny into the family room, she explained to the family what was going on.

"Wow, Aunt Jill. You have got a better memory than I do. I only remember a few of them," Charlie said rubbing his brow.

"Well, I've got more years than you do." He looked up at her astonished.

"Then was there any that had strange deaths?" Charlie asked.

"Define strange. Oh, wait a minute," Jill paused, "There were a few."

"Only a few? Well, that may narrow down the search," Jeremy said.

"Who did he look like?" Jill asked Jeremy.

"Charlie."

"I see what you mean. That could be anyone."

"Okay. That answers my question," Charlie said, "Who wants to go to the library?" Jenny and David decided to go, and Alex left for the day. Jeremy had other things in mind.

Michael came walking into the barn, this time to see if the spirit was there. But he had already left and Fireball was nibbling on a couple of carrots left on the floor.

"Hey boy," he said as he rubbed his neck, "I know you must really be confused." Fireball looked up at him as if he was about to say something, but kept chewing.

"You've seen him again huh?" The horse kind of nodded at him. "I am just as baffled as you are. There is more than one person who this could be, and no one has seen him yet either." At that point, Fireball nodded yea. "Oh really? What did I miss? Boy, I am slacking off my job here. I will find out," Michael said before he turned around and left. Fireball had already gotten used to Michael coming around to see him. There were times when Michael would carry on a full conversation with Fireball. His advantage was that he could also read the horses' mind.

After arriving at the library, they went straight to the newspaper archive section to look on the computers available. All three sat down at different computer and began searching through the archived newspapers online. Charlie looked through the last ten years as David and Jenny browsed through the previous twenty and forty years. After a couple of hours David pulled up one that showed an article about a car accident that happened not far from the race track. Then he saw a picture of the relative of Charlie who looked just like him except for the build. He was short, yet a light weight physique.

"Hey Charlie, look at this. Do you think this is him? Charlie rolled over to look at it.

"Yea, he looks familiar. Mom said he was in a car accident after the big race that day. That was at least forty years ago."

"Ok. I will print this picture out along with the article."

"Okay." They also printed out other pictures and articles to take home with them.

When they had returned home, Charlie discovered from Jill that Jeremy had gone to meet Caroline for coffee.

"That figures. No wonder he did not want to come."

After picking up Caroline, Jeremy drove through a drive up at a coffee shop for coffee before they went for a drive.

"Do you like going to the beach?" Jeremy asked.

"Yea, that's a great idea. That is one of my favorite spots to go," she said as she waved her hand through the wind in the open top jeep.

When they arrived at the beach, they started walking by the water's edge. Little did they know that Michael, his guardian angel, was walking along with them.

"So, what do you do for fun?" he asked.

"I enjoy doing the races and training the horses with my dad. I am going to start being the jockey for my own horse." That took Jeremy back for a moment.

"Wow! Uh…That's cool," he said cooly, but in the back of his mind, he was wondering, "Uh oh, what am I thinking?"

"We race for a cause for the Childrens Foundation on the island. What are y'all going to be racing for?" Michael put a thought in his ear.

"Well, I've been pondering over that myself. We are a Christian family. We are usually in church on Sunday mornings. That is something we need do discuss as a family."

They got to know each other during the rest of the time they spent on the beach. By the time he returned home, he found everyone in the family room talking and waiting for him.

"So how was your date?" Charlie asked as Jeremy strolled into the room and plopped down in his favorite big chair.

"It was nice."

"Do you realize that their horses could easily beat Fireball in any race?"

"Oh yes, I know. But I also found out that they are also racing for a cause, the Children's Foundation. Guys, I think we need to do this too. You know, not just for the money."

"Wow!" David said, "Is this the same Jeremy we know? What did you do with the real Jeremy?"

"Yea man. I know. At first, I was thinking of myself. But she helped me realize that racing for a cause is also more meaningful."

"That's cool," Charlie said, "Remember? We have got a mystery to figure out too. We brought back some pictures for you to look at," Charlie said handing him the pictures. He began browsing through them.

"Nope, nope, maybe, maybe," he said thumbing through the pictures, "Whoa. Wait a minute. These three kind of look familiar." Jeremy gave them back to Charlie.

"Okay. At least we have something to go on." Charlie told everyone about the background of the final three. "This one is dad's third cousin, Glenn, who died in 1921," he said showing the picture, "He married twelve years before his death. This one is Uncle George, who was my dad's brother who died in 1937. And this is Joseph Ralph Gordon, a third cousin to me. He married Aunt Juliette, who is also related to Aunt Jill." That got Jenny's attention. Then he went on. "That would have been Jenny's great Aunt Julia, as she like to be called. And he died around 1950. All three of these were jockeys for their own horses."

"I see. So, what do we do now?" Jeremy asked. Michael was present during the family discussion.

"You need to talk to the closest relatives," Michael said to Jeremy. Jeremy immediately repeated what Michael said.

"Quick thinking," David said, "Now we need to do some calling. But you know they are going to ask why."

"We will just tell them that we are doing some research on the jockeys in the family. And find out more about the names of the horses they were training and racing. You know, like how they died and what were their missions in life were." Michael also put a bug in Jeremy's ear. "What were their relationships like and their faith walk?" Jeremy immediately looked over his shoulder and realized that it was Michael talking to him.

"Huh? Okay. What about their relationships and faith walk?"

"Where did you get that from?" Charlie asked.

"Their whole family has been in some kind of ministry," Jill said.

"Oh really?" Jenny asked. "I didn't know that."

Everyone had someone to call. Jill had some ideas of where the relatives lived and she had some of their telephone numbers with her. Jeremy went outside onto the porch and sat down in the swing for a while. Just as he sat down, Michael was standing against the post nearby.

"There you are! Do you know what is going on? Or are you going to make me work for this one?"

"I am checking into this also my friend. Try to catch up with this spirit and see if you can possibly talk to him if you can."

"Yeah. That might be easier said than done."

"Oh? Like going for coffee with Caroline?"

"I know you were there. I heard you."

"And what will your cause be for? Have you thought about that? Remember, it is the ministry that your family is based on."

"I am not sure yet. But it's got to be for something special."

"That is right. Let it be for something that is close to and the heart of the family. Think about what your aunt would want."

"I get it. I need to think about this and ask Jenny," Jeremy said looking down. Yet when he looked up, Michael was gone. "I hate it when he does that."

Meanwhile, the spirit appeared by Fireball's stall. He kind of startled him for the horse was nibbling on a carrot.

"Whoa boy. It's okay. I have got something to talk to you about." Then he had Fireball's full attention.

"You're going to be racing for something special." And Fireball gave him a funny look.

"There is something that is special to Aunt Jessie's heart. I know that much." Fireball said, "Something in town that she had started a long time ago,"

"Well, little dude," Michael said, "Let us put some energy into your spunk for winning these races coming up. We do not want to let those others knock you out of the race. Now do we?"

Fireball shook his head, "No not this dude." Not long after he left, Alex came into the barn.

"Come on, boy. Let's get some exercise." Alex saddled him up and was about to take him out to the meadow when Jeremy came in.

"Hey Alex," Jeremy said, "Let me do it this time."

"Are you sure about that?"

"Yeah, I'm sure," he said taking the reins from him, "I feel like I need to get used to doing this once for all."

"Right. Good time like the present."

Alex held the reigns while Jeremy got up in the saddle. Fireball looked around at him as if he was thinking "Are you sure about this?"

"Yeah, Fireball. I am sure about this. Remember, we are a team." Alex led them to the meadow back behind the rose garden and behind the swing. There were a few obstacles already set up within the area.

"Okay Fireball. Let's show him what you've got." Alex said as he handed the reigns up to Jeremy.

"I'm ready if you are," Jeremy said patting his neck. Before he knew, Fireball took off and left Alex in a cloud of dust.

They rode around the meadow that expanded out at least five acres or more almost as big as the race track. Once Jeremy got his grip, he finally got control of the direction to go around the obstacle course for now. After a few rounds, Jeremy led him through the course and was able to stay on.

"Good boy," he said, as they were in a gallop.

"I got this," he heard Fireball say, or was he hearing the horses' thoughts, "Yea man, we're a team."

"Am I hearing you right?" Jeremy asked.

"Oh yea, it took you long enough to get the nerve to come play," Fireball said as he

"Really?" Jeremy was kind of shocked, "Can anyone else hear you?"

"No dude. Just you."

"How is that? I do not get it," he said as they walked near the edge of the forest.

"It's okay man. You are my compadre ."

The sun was starting to go down, And Jeremy brought him to the edge of the forest where the beach lay not too far from where they were. As they came out onto the sandy beach, Jeremy could see some of the late afternoon walkers and joggers still out. Alex followed them down to the beach. One of the things that Alex enjoyed was riding horses, but this was special, for it is the first time he noticed was that Jeremy and Fireball had a special connection. It was like they were meant to be like family. It wasn't long, when Jeremy got off Fireball, and they walked along the beach at the water's edge.

"It's good to see that you guys actually get along," Alex said to Jeremy.

"Yeah! He kind of surprised me too."

"It's like you two were meant to be."

Jeremy and Alex took off their shoes and socks and set them down on the sand. He began to wade into the water for a little way until he was almost knee high. He got off Fireball and they were walking in the water. For a minute, Fireball just realized that Jeremy wasn't guiding him by the reigns. Fireball started following Jeremy and Alex into the water wading around in the cool freshness that splashed up against them. Jeremy went a little deeper to where he was almost waist deep. When Fireball got a little closer, he turned around and splashed him. It startled Fireball and took him off guard. Before Jeremy knew it, Fireball was chasing him around the water. Alex was laughing at them from the edge of the water. By the time Jeremy thought he could side swipe the horse, he lost his balance and fell into the water. Before he realized it, he was drenched, and Fireball let out one of his crazy yells like he was laughing at him.

"Okay. You got me back. Are you having fun now?" Jeremy asked?

"Yeah! This is fun!" Fireball said to him.

"Now you know how to have fun, little dude," he said even though Alex was watching.

Fireball waded a little deeper and just laid out in the water not far from Jeremy.

"Well, I guess that is a Yep," Alex said from the edge. Alex was surprised how funny Fireball could be. Now he understood what Jeremy meant by 'You never know what he's going to do next' as he was just like Jeremy. Alex was laughing at them both. "Fireball, I think the family's craziness is rubbing off on you." Jeremy kind of grinned about that.

"Yeah, he's part of the family" Jeremy said as he waded out of the water.

They noticed that some of the others on the beach were enjoying the sight of them playing in the water. Fireball came out of the water when a short woman came up to him and rubbed his neck. "I wish I had a horse like you."

"He's not quite ready to start a family yet," Jeremy said

"Why is that? Oh, you are still a young fella, aren't you?" she asked Fireball. And Fireball rubbed up against her sort of pushing her around. "You're playful too."

"That he is," Jeremy said reaching down to grab his now wet shoes, "Oh darn it. I might as well wait for these." The young woman laughed at him as he crawled back up into the saddle with Alex on the side.

"See you around," Alex said as they were turning Fireball around towards the forest.

"Yea, maybe I'll see you another time," she said waving at them as they rode off.

Before they got to the thicket of the forest, Alex was able to get his shoes back on before getting into the path. After they approached the meadow, Jeremy reached down and patted Fireball's neck.

"You enjoyed that. Didn't you?" Jeremy felt like he needed to get down for a few minutes to walk a little bit, so he dismounted after getting his shoes back on. Almost after he got down to the cool grass, Fireball had to do a full body shake that shook off the rest of the droplets of water from his coat. Fireball rose up off the ground and let out a 'Hallelujah' neigh. When Jeremy failed to catch the reigns, Fireball let out across the meadow leaving Jeremy and Alex behind and dumbfounded. They just looked at each other.

"Hey!" they yelled, "Wait for us." They started running to catch up with their unpredictable friend. They were half-way when they noticed that Fireball had taken a U-turn and was racing back towards them.

"Whoa, boy, wait a minute." Jeremy said waving his hands. Fireball side swiped him and knocked him down for the second time.

"Hey, that is not fair. You got me at a disadvantage," he said sitting in the grass and Alex was laughing at him. Then here comes Fireball walking up beside them and nudged Jeremy on his shoulder, and just stood there. It seemed like he was saying 'Gotcha!"

"Yea, you got me good," he said as he grabbed the reins and stood up. "Do you think we can make it the rest of the way now?" Fireball looked around at him, but stood still long enough for Jeremy to mount up again. At first, Jeremy was almost expecting something out of the ordinary that Fireball might pull. This time Fireball decided to play nice.

"Thank you," Jeremy said to him. They rode the rest of the way towards the back of the house where they saw Jenny and David sitting in the swing laughing at them. And Alex was not far behind walking over to them.

"He got you alright. Jeremy? I thought you were afraid to ride Fireball," Jenny asked a they rode up toward them.

"At first, yeah. It just took me a long time to get the nerve up to do this. But hey, we did it. Right? Boy?" he said to Fireball as he was nodding his head.

"He had fun at the beach," Alex said, "You should've seen him."

"Fireball? What happened?"

"Let's say he's a crowd pleaser," Alex said.

"And a show-off," Jeremy added.

"We've got a crazy horse, don't we?"

"Yep. That's Fireball. David said, "I think he loves the attention. He is nothing like the other horses. He has got a unique character of his own. Right? Jeremy?"

"Yep, "

"Crazy is the word," Alex said as Fireball looked over at him. "Okay. Don't' make me say it."

Jenny looks at him, "What's that?"

"You know. It is the 'Jeremy' saying, 'Don't give me that look." And they started laughing, even Jeremy.

Chantilly, Fireballs' mom, was loose in the back yard. They would let her roam the back yard sometimes as a chance for her to see Fireball and be around the family. Chantilly came up beside Jeremy and put her chin on Jeremy's shoulder, and his reaction was priceless.

The following morning, arrived early to meet the others outside the barn.

"Hey boy. Let's go get your morning exercise. It is time to get serious about this." Fireball was prancing around and ready to get out of his stall, "Come on," Alex said opening the gate, "We're going to the track to work on your speed."

A friend of Alex's met them at the track along with Charlie and David. Alex made a few rounds on the track with Fireball before another horse and its rider came out, He came up beside them.

"Ready?"

"Yes, I believe we're ready," Alex said. Charlie blew his whistle, and they were off. David was watching in anticipation. The horses were running almost side by side; and then Alex whispered something in his ear. Fireball almost instantly started speeding up. The other horse tried to stay up with him but Fireball kept going faster and faster; and he was way ahead when he crossed the finish line. Charlie came over to them and patted his nose, "Good boy, I knew you had it in you. You are running like we did for mama's homemade biscuits."

"Hey Alex, what did you whisper to him?" David asked.

"Just a little nudge of advice," Alex said. And then they saw Caroline riding out on Firecracker. Fireball looked around and noticed who it was. She rode up beside them.

"Hi Fireball," Caroline said, "We're going to make this tough for you."

Charlie rubbed his nose, "Okay, boy. I want you to remember what Alex told you." Fireball seemed to be looking straight at Charlie. They lined up the horses and Charlie blew his whistle. They were off in a cloud of dust. This time Fireball was running faster than the first time with the other horse. They were not even halfway when he started moving further ahead of Firecracker. This surprised Caroline. He didn't even look back, so Alex kept urging him on. Fireball was almost like in flight when he had passed the finish line; he broke his first record time. The guys were surprised and let out a yell of celebration. Caroline came riding up to Alex. "What in the world changed his mind?"

"Oh just a little bit of convincing," he said smiling.

"Looks like I'm going to have some good competition now." She was also happy for Fireball. As they were beside each other, Firecracker looked over at Fireball as she was licking her lips saying to him "Okay. You win this time."

The next couple of days, Fireball got his exercise and plus extra laps around the track to help him pick up his speed. Tuesday afternoon while they were doing the laps around the track, Jeremy noticed the spirit up in the stands. So, he started up the steps going up toward where he was at. At first, Jeremy thought he might disappear by the time he reached him; but suddenly, he was right there beside him.

"Hi Jeremy. How are you doing?"

"Huh? So, you are just now coming around to talk to us now?"

"Oh, not just yet, my boy. I have got business to do with that Fireball first. I just thought it might be nice of me to let you know that I will get around to that also," he said in a quant English accent.

"Oh really? And how come you will not talk to Michael?" Jeremy asked referring to the Angel.

"I'm sorry Jeremy. But it does not always work that way," the man said then disappeared before his eyes.

"Dang it," Jeremy said "Why didn't I get his name?" Jeremy stood there for a moment and stomped his foot. Then he turned around and proceeded back down the steps of the grand stand. Charlie came over to him as he came closer to the bottom.

"That was him?"

"Yeah. But I did not get his name. Darn it."

"Maybe we'll catch up with him later," Charlie said. Charlie couldn't make out who it was at a distance. He was wondering who this could be, and why is he coming around now.

"He did tell me that he has business with Fireball first. I guess he will eventually come to us soon," Jeremy said.

"Wouldn't we all."

Meanwhile, back at the house, Jenny was coming out of the bathroom for the third time and met her mom in the hall.

"You've got morning sickness," she said.

"No, it cannot be. Can it?"

"Sweetheart, the only way we're going to find out is go to the doctor."

Jenny gave her a look, "You think I'm pregnant?"

"Come on dear. Let's go now."

The guys got back home from the track an hour later and unloaded Fireball before heading for the house. They stopped at the porch, and Jeremy made himself comfortable in the swing as the others were either leaning on a post or up against the house.

"You know what guys. We need to decide on what kind of charity we are going to use for our mission," Charlie said. They were quietly thinking it over when Jenny and her mom drove up. She got out of the car, came over to David and gave him a big kiss in front of the others.

"Wow! What is this for?" he asked as he was holding her.

"You'll never guess," she said smiling.

Jeremy stood up, "I know. You are pregnant!" he shouted. Jenny just smiled.

"Are you really?" David asked.

"Yes dear. We are going to have a baby," she said glowing.

Everyone was so happy for them. Rosa even cooked a special lunch for them.

When they gathered around the table, Jeremy sat beside his sister.

"I knew it. I knew it. It has been a whole week and a half since you started having morning sickness. But now you are going to have to eat more healthy foods."

"How is it I didn't catch on to that?" David asked.

"Brother, you've been busy thinking about what else has been going on lately," Jeremy said as Charlie agreed.

"Don't worry about that," Rosa said. "I'll make sure that she eats a balance diet." Rosa had finished laying out an array of different dishes on the table.

"Are you hungry for all this?" David asked.

"Just hungry," she said sliding the dish of roasted chicken toward her plate. "Do not worry dear. The doctor already talked to me about my diet. I've got it covered."

"That's it!" Jeremy said.

"What's it?" Jenny asked.

"We could start a mission for the mothers and children of the island."

"That's what mom used to do," Charlie said dishing out some steamed vegetables onto his plate.

"There is a place on the island that mom used to support. I am going to check it out after lunch."

"That's a good idea, Jeremy," David said, "Leave it to you to figure that out."

"Now I know why this spirits' conversing with Fireball first," Jeremy said.

"Really?" Jenny asked, "It would be nice if only Fireball can talk to us and fill us in on what's going on."

After lunch, Charlie called the organization they were talking about.

"Well, guys, we got a problem," he said after the conversation, "There was so much that mom left to this organization in her will. I remember now."

"Well, that is good. But what's the problem?"

"Mom was head of the board for this organization and she did have an active role in working with them."

"What's the name of it?" David asked as they all gathered in the family room.

"They were in the process of doing that when mom died, but they are not quite sure what the organization's name was going to be. It was something between 'New Horizons' or 'Beginnings.' We need to make the decision on this and do the final paperwork."

Everyone was quiet for a few minutes. Jill was the one to break the silence.

"I would like to call a vote for 'New Horizons.' It just seems to have a ring to it." They all agreed to that one.

"Of course we could also add, 'in the honor of Jessie Gordon'" Jenny said.

Michael silently agreed to that as he heard the whole conversation while he was standing not far from the chair where Jeremy was sitting. Then he tapped Jeremy on his shoulder. When he almost looked over his shoulder, Michael mentioned something in his ear.

"Guys," Jeremy said, "I think we better make a visit there to see if there is anything else that's needed." They gazed at him for a moment. Charlie was almost out of his chair reaching for his keys when everyone else followed suit.

They arrived later at the organization in two different vehicles.

"Hey Charlie," Doris, the office manager said meeting them in the lobby. "It's so good to see you," she said as she gave him a hug.

"Hi Doris. So how are things going around here? Are you holding down the fort?"

"Oh yes, and so much more," she said with a half-smile.

"Oh?"

"You would not believe what's going on. Two of my people are out sick, and there is more to do than we have enough of help."

"Okay," Charlie said, "What can we do to help?"

"Well, Jenny. I know you are a nurse. Could you please help those out in the children's clinic?"

"Why yes I can." Jenny left and went to the ward, to help with the children who would come in sick with families of limited funds in the household. Before they knew it, everyone was helping with something. Mrs. Doris had two of the guys moving around medical beds into different areas of the building.

"Charlie I'm separating the two different sections to where one side of the building is for the children; and of course, the other side is for the mothers and fathers."

"That's a good idea," he said also realizing that it was still a one floor building. He stopped for a moment and sent a text to Jenny.

"Do we need more space or beds?"

"Well, I don't quite know where we'd put them," Doris said waving her hand.

He looked at his text from Jenny and showed it to Jeremy. All he had to do was shake his head.

"I believe it's time to expand up and out," Doris was beaming when she said, "That would be wonderful. I know we have got the room to add on here. As you know, we are on five acres here."

"Yes, and we would still have plenty area for parking too. My brother-in-law, David, will be the perfect person to get this started. He can whip together the plans in no time for us to really expand. And we will add two more floors also, so we will have plenty of room."

"That's great! You know, we will also need to double or triple our staff here."

"That is okay Mrs. Doris. We will work on that together."

"So, what have you decided for the organizations' name? We have had that sign 'Mothers and Children Welcome' for quite a while now." It was six years ago when Jessie gave Mrs. Doris for proposition to be over the organization. Doris and her husband were missionaries looking for something special to work on together when they were approached by Jessie for the job. Her husband, Reverend Harold Barclay, started having daily services that were inspiring to those who came to the mid-day meetings. It was a great way of bringing the families together. Even people from other businesses close by came over on their lunch breaks for the short services before returning to work.

"New Horizons," Jeremy said, "And why stop there? I think the whole family should be welcome."

"That's right," Charlie said as he agreed. "This is a family-oriented organization."

"I agree with you on that, and I like that name 'New Horizons.' Your mom would be so proud of all of you."

"We've got a lot to do, don't we?' Charlie asked. By the end of the day, Jill was able to hire three new people to add to their staff. That evening, the conversation around the dinner table was quite interesting. David was drawing out the building plan on his writing tablet and talking to Charlie about different ideas.

Jenny, Jill, and Roger were discussing an ad to put in the local paper and possibilities of how the new sign would look to put at the front of the property.

And Jeremy was working on his schedule with Alex for working with Fireball to get him ready for the next race that would be about a week away.

"So, I guess we don't worry about that spirit right now?" Alex asked him.

"Only temporarily. It seems like he has got plans for Fireball now. He is not out of the picture though. I do wish someone could help us out on this," Jeremy said as he was really referring to Michael, who was present in the room as he listened in to all the conversation around the table.

"In time my friend," Michael said, "I cannot do this for you. But you do know I am here to guide you."

Jeremy thought for a moment that he did hear Michael.

"I'm going to try talking to him again real soon," Jeremy said.

"Good idea. The rest of this week is going to be busy for us and Fireball as well. At least he is not fooling around for now."

"Do not bet on it. You know how Fireball is."

"True. Very true," Alex said looking up to see Rosa walking in with desert. Everyone stopped talking to see what kind of surprise she had for them.

"Oh, it's strawberry cake," Charlie said, "My favorite."

"I knew you'd like this as you are embarking in new horizons," she said smiling.

"I like the way you put that," Jenny said.

"You know this was also Jessie's favorite too. Well, besides tea cakes."

"Thank you, Rosa," Charlie said as he was putting slices on saucers for everyone. One of the things that Charlie always enjoyed was serving the desert to his family. It was a tradition in their family for the men or head of household to serve desert. And even though Rosa had been working for them; Jessie always insisted on helping her with dinner. Jessie used to always enjoy cooking. It was one of her favorite things to do for it gave her the chance to chat with Rosa. Jessie considered her a part of their family because Rosa lost her mom at a young age.

The following morning David called a construction company in town to discuss his plans and he set up the following week to begin renovations on the building. As for Charlie and Jenny, they started doing some extra research of the three possible relatives of who the anonymous spirit might be.

The rest of the week, Fireball got his daily exercise and laps around the track. Jenny and Jill later went to the local newspaper to put in the ads for personnel for 'New Horizons,' and they also put in an ad for local support for their new endeavor.

The beginning of the next week rolled around before they knew it. Monday morning, David was already at 'New Horizons' when Able Construction crew showed up to began work on the building.

Mrs. Doris had gotten a call from the Medical Clinic down the road, and Dr. Smith, the Head doctor, came by to talk to her. He gave her an offer that she could not refuse. He said that their clinic would be happy to accept 'New Horizons' patients with the same low fees to help her out. She was so thrilled to get the news.

"Mrs. Doris, I know it'll take a few weeks before you'll get everything back up and running."

"And I do appreciate this very much," she said. "My crew will most definitely be there to pitch in to also help you keep up with your regular patients."

When race day came around on Thursday, Fireball was more than ready. Alex was set up and ready when the riders were getting positioned at the gates. He looked over to see that Firecracker was also there with Caroline as the rider this time. As the bell sounded, they were off and running. They were halfway when Fireball had already caught up with Firecracker. They were running side by side for the longest minute.

"Are we going to do this again?" Alex asked him

Fireball eyed the beauty beside him, then noticed that she was inching her way ahead of him. Then before Alex knew it, Fireball took off like a lightning bolt. He crossed the finish line far ahead of Firecracker which took Caroline by surprise. When the announcer was sharing the winner over the speaker, he also mentioned that all proceeds were going to the renovations of 'New Horizons.'

"That's awesome!" Charlie said as he patted Fireball on his neck and gave him an apple.

"Hey Fireball," Caroline said riding over to the excited crowd around them and Alex turned him around.

"He did a great job," she said smiling, "Now he's in for the run of the trophy."

"Thanks," Alex said, "I wish I knew what got into him. But he is very impressive."

"Yes, he is indeed," Caroline said as she noticed Jeremy at the edge of the crowd. She had dismounted and walked over to him with her horse.

"How are you doing, Jeremy?"

"I am doing okay. We've all been busy with everything lately. It's good to see you out there riding. I know you enjoy that."

"Yes, I do. If you have got time later today, would you like to go for a ride to the beach?"

"Well," Jeremy said looking at his watch," I think that is possible for a little while this afternoon. I will be in touch."

"Okay, I will talk to you later. Come on Firecracker," she said to her horse, "We've got to get you cleaned up girl." Caroline walked off with Firecracker as Jeremy watched them leave the track.

"Hey Jeremy," David said to Jeremy breaking his gaze, "You have actually got a thing for her. Don't you?"

"Umm, I'm not quite sure yet. But she is quite a beauty, isn't she?"

"Do you mean her or the horse?"

"Hey, that's not funny," Jeremy said slapping him on the shoulder. Jenny came up beside David.

"Did you see that look in his eyes? I really think he's falling for her," she said after Jeremy had started walking towards the horse stalls.

"Yea, that is the first time I've seen him look at a woman like that."

It was in the late afternoon after they all had returned home, when Jeremy was sitting outside on the swing in the rose garden. He was gazing out across the meadow. Charlie came walking up and sat down by him.

"A penny for your thoughts." He was quiet for a moment. Charlie looked over at him.

"What's wrong?"

"I feel like I'm always praying for forgiveness."

"What on earth for?"

"All the stupid things I've done," Jeremy said waving his hand around.

"Are you talking about what happened three years ago?"

"Well, uh, yeah. I did not really have any intentions to hurt anyone at the time. I guess I just let other things get in the way."

"Jeremy, man. Hear me out," Charlie said kind of turning toward him, "Mom knew in her heart that you were not that kind of person. When she hugged you; that was her way of saying 'You are forgiven. It is okay.' You are a part of this family. Get used to it."

"Yeah, I know. I just wish I could go back and change things."

"Like how you hooked up with that broad? She talked you into that. Didn't' she?"

"Oh yeah. I know. Don't remind me," Jeremy said sitting back, "I cannot believe I did that. And she was not really my type either."

"Jeremy, do not beat yourself up over that. We all make mistakes. That's how we learn and grow. The race we run in life should never be compared to the next person. I am not going to sit here and judge you. Where would that get me?" Charlie asked.

"Do not know. All I know is that I want to do better. I could sure use a little guidance along the way."

"Let go of the past," Charlie said, "As your cousin, I urge you to set your eyes toward the future, toward your own faith. Let us run the race of life that has been set before us with perseverance and the hope that our ancestors taught us."

"That's true. You know what? You are right Charlie. I can do this," Jeremy said getting up after patting Charlie on his shoulder. Jeremy walked inside and went to his room. He remembered something that rang a bell to him while Charlie was talking to him. He sat down on his bed, and looked around.

"Where did I put that?" He looked through the drawers and under the bed. Then he walked over to a chair that was by the window and sat down. The moment he sat down, he saw it sitting right where he laid it the last time on the round table by the chair. He opened the Bible, flipping through the different books. "Not the Old Testament. I know it is in the New Testament." After a few minutes of thumbing through the pages, he came to Hebrews twelve. "That's it!" He read it and read it again for it to sink in. "Let us run with perseverance the race that is set before us. We do this by keeping our eyes on Jesus on whom our faith depends from start to finish."

"Wow! It is God's will for us all to win the race of life! Thank you, Charlie," he said to himself, "I needed that." Then he took time to bring himself into his quiet place for prayer and meditation, "Lord, I am not perfect. I never will be. But I keep trying to do better every day you give me life. I need your help, Lord. Please help me to be the kind of person you want me to be. I want to be more like you, my Lord and Savior. Amen." Jeremy did not realize that Michael was also present in the room just watching and listening quietly. The one thing that startled Jeremy was his cell phone.

"Hello. Uh. Oh, hey Caroline." There was a pause and then he said, "Let us do that another day. I hope you don't mind. I have got some things I need to take care of. Okay?" and then he hung up.

As he went running down the stairs, Jeremy was looking for Jenny or David. When he could not find them or anyone else, he figured everyone was busy doing something. So, he went outside for a walk and he walked all the way through the meadow, past the forest, to the beach. As he approached the beach, he thought someone was following him at first as he glanced around a couple of times to see nothing. He finally stopped and sat down on a big rock not far from the shore.

"Jeremy," he heard his name and looked around. No one was there. "Jeremy" the voice said again. He thought for a moment that it was Michael, but it was not his voice.

"Okay. I do not see you, but I hear you," then he calmed down and thought "Is it you Lord? I am here and I am listening." Everything was quiet around him, but the sounds of the birds and the waves on the shore.

"It is okay, Jeremy. You have been forgiven many times over, the Lord said.

"Thank you," he said with a big sigh of relief. "This isn't easy, you know."

"When you emptied your heart to me, you also opened the door for me," the Lord said.

"Oh? Okay. Am I doing something wrong again?" Jeremy asked as he kind of looked around then just decided to focus on the waves beating upon the sand and making ripples.

"No, my son," the Lord said, "But I have something for you to do. I think you know what it is."

"The spirit?" he guessed.

"That's right. You must ask him what is your next step, and he will tell you everything you need to know."

"Me? Why is it he only talks to me? I don't understand."

"Yes you. This is something that you must do for yourself. This is where your journey will take you."

"Well, uh. Okay," he said as he noticed someone walking by and probably wondering who he was talking to. Then he turned back to face the ocean. "Okay. I know what I must do."

Then he was alone again. Jeremy sat there wondering what in the world this could be about. Before he realized it, he was not walking, but running back towards the house. He was very anxious to try to talk to the spirit. He walked into the barn to check on Fireball. But Fireball was not alone. The spirit was there visiting with Fireball. Instead of waiting this time, Jeremy walked right over to him.

"Are you expecting him to answer you?" he asked.

"No, but I know what he's thinking," he said turning to Jeremy. "Like you also know what he's thinking also."

"Okay. At least you are talking to me now."

"You have a question for me?"

"Yes, what is it that I'm supposed to do?" Jeremy asked.

"You do know that Fireball is your horse. Don't you?"

"Well, uh, no. I did not know that? How?"

"Jessie left it in her will that the filly of Chantilly would be yours. Charlie did not want to scare you about this."

"He knows? Well, uh, no I am not really scared. I'm just a little confused. He listens to me even since I have been training him. I have kind of gotten used to him now. Why?"

"He probably thought that if you knew, you'd be afraid of the responsibility of taking care of him until you were ready."

"That's cool dude," Fireball chimed in, "That's my compadre." Jeremy laughed about this. "Yeah. And we are always picking at each other."

"It's like 'we' were meant to be," Fireball raised his head in excitement.

"Is there anything else I should know?"

"Yes, son. That means you should also consider being the rider of your own horse."

"Me? Well, uh, what do I need to do?" Jeremy asked getting anxious.

"Do not fret my boy. Charlie and Alex can help you with that. And yes, you are the right size and light weight also," the spirit said rubbing Fireballs nose. Fireball let out a sound as if he already knew that.

"Wow! We do get along pretty good. Well, most of the time."

"Yeah. And besides the picking that goes on between you two." Both Jeremy and Fireball gave him a funny look. It was like 'Wow! This dude was reading their minds.'

"Well, you guys got practice to do now." And he was about to leave.

"Wait a minute," Jeremy said, "what's your name?"

"Joseph Ralph Gordon. I was the owner of Tornado," he said smiling; "Now you can tell Michael it's okay."

"I never understood how you guys operate," Jeremy said.

"My boy, we call it the honor system," Joseph said before he faded out of view. Jeremy looks at Fireball.

"Well, Fireball, it looks like we've got work to do, right?" This time Fireball totally agreed with him when he shook his head and held his tail high and proud to be his horse. Jeremy opened the stall gate and saddled up Fireball.

"Wait a minute," Fireball said, "You might want to back up." So, he did. And Fireball danced around yelling and neighing "Woo hoo. For he was letting out his excitement and going in circles.

"Okay. Settle down now," Jeremy said grabbing the reins. This time Fireball was being more cooperative with him. Once in the saddle, they rode around the corral a few times and then they came outside the barn. Jeremy rode him around the back yard and then into the meadow.

"Fireball," he said as they were at the edge of the meadow and he got more settled into the saddle, "Do you think we can take this slow at first?" Fireball kind of looked around at him was about fifteen minutes after riding in circles around the meadow when he noticed Charlie standing at the edge of the meadow watching them. Jeremy rode over to him and slowed down to a stop.

"Hey" Charlie said, "Looks like you're doing pretty good with him."

"Yes Jeremy. He is legally yours. I guess the spirit told you?"

"Yes, he did. And he's Joseph Ralph Gordon. He was the owner of Tornado. Right?"

"Yep, that's right. I didn't want to tell you too soon because I wasn't quite sure how you'd react," Charlie said and saw the expression on Jeremy's face. "Does this mean that you're ready to be his rider?"

"You betcha," Jeremy said sitting up proudly in the saddle, "Maybe we can start working on this at the track."

"You got it bro. I am very pleased that's what you want to do. We will meet Alex there first thing in the morning."

"Sounds great to me," Jeremy said as he turned around and they made a few more rounds before heading for the barn. As he passed Chantilly's stall next to Fireball's, her head went up in surprise. He dismounted and proceeded to take the saddle and blanket off. Fireball voluntarily walked into his stall and turned around to see that Jeremy had already given him some food. As Jeremy shut the gate, he heard behind him.

"You ride like a champ," Joseph said.

"It is just a start. But I'm going to keep his mind on the racing and getting his exercise in," Jeremy said turning around.

"That's very good to hear. I was hoping you would say that."

"Well, it's kind of been like a wakeup call. I'm attached to this young one." Fireball gave him an expression with his ears cocked back saying "I'm listening to my owner."

"How do you mean?" he heard Michael ask somewhere from the side. Jeremy looked around to be surprised it was Michael.

"You found your way to where you should be?" Michael asked. Jeremy just realized that Joseph had already left the scene.

"Yeah, you could say that. And I see now why you are not supposed to help. Some things we just must learn on our own."

"That's correct. I can guide you and give you advice. But I can't make that decision for you. You must do that for yourself. The 'Great One' always guides people through others."

"I see what you mean," Jeremy said sliding his foot through the dust on the floor. He looked down now and when he glanced up,

Michael was gone. So, Jeremy finally said good-night to Fireball and went inside.

That evening at dinner, everyone was excited to hear the good news about Jeremy. Jenny was sitting beside him as usual.

"I'm proud of you," Jenny said, patting his hand, and he held her hand temporarily.

"Sis, now I know where my journey is going."

She was happy for him and reached over and gave him a hug. "Remember, its how you run the race that encourages others around you," she said as she picked up her fork again.

"I know that now."

"Yeah brother. Even if it's through the way you make people laugh. You are unique in your own way. We just want to see you happy too.," Charlie said.

"I guess I got that from dad's side of the family," he said as it got Roger's attention,

"How do you think I got your mothers attention when we first met?" Roger said smiling at Jill.

"Sweetheart, you were the clown in the group," Jill said.

"And the one most likely to succeed in making people smile," then he turned his attention back to Jeremy, "I'm proud of you Jeremy."

"Thanks for stepping in and being a father to me. That means a lot to me," Jeremy said reaching for an extra helping of carrots. Jeremy also told everyone who the spirit really was.

"You were probably the only one he needed to talk to after all," Charlie said.

"I guess so. So, I reckon we'll soon see for sure." Jeremy said.

The following morning, Jenny was coming down the stairs to go help Rosa when she missed a step and landed on the floor, Rosa heard her scream and came running in. She came and kneeled beside her and noticed Jenny could not move her right foot.

"Jenny!" Rosa said, "Do not move. What hurts?" she asked then also called for David and her mom.

"Ouch. I think I twisted my ankle," she said when the others came down the stairs.

"Oh no! How did you land sweetie?" Jill asked.

"Oh great. I might have hit my stomach."

Charlie and Jeremy had already left to go to the race track to practice and Alex met them there. He showed him how his stance should be when he is racing and after going a couple rounds, he rode up.

"How'd I do this time?"

"You are doing better. You're going to beat me out of a job," Alex said.

"Not in this lifetime," Charlie said, "We're keeping you on as his trainer."

"Okay. Jeremy. This time, let's go for it and we will time you," Alex said.

"I'm ready," he said as he got into position. Charlie blew his whistle and Jeremy was gone before he finished and went flying around the track. Both were shocked as they looked at each other. When he got back around to the finish line, they were totally impressed.

"Wow!" Charlie said looking at his stop watch, "You are light on your feet, Fireball. Impressive."

"Yeah, he goes faster with you. How did you do that?"

"Don't ask me. Ask him," Jeremy said as Fireball seemed to be in good spirits.

"Fireball, you're been holding out on me," Alex said.

Without Jeremy guiding him around, Fireball pranced around in a circle like he was pleased with himself and he held his tail high. "Hey yes, I'm happy."

"Whoa boy," Jeremy said, "I know you're excited now," he said taking hold of the reins and pulling back a little.

"You guys are a team," Alex said, "That means he'll work with you more than ever now."

"Yeah, that's good to know," Jeremy took a few more laps around the track when Charlie had to answer his phone.

"Huh? What happened?" he asked as Alex heard him talking, "Okay. Keep me posted. We will be here a little longer."

The doctor came over to David and the family in the waiting room as David stood up.

"How is she doing? Is the baby okay?"

"She lucky. The baby is okay. However, I had to put her foot in a temporary cast to let it heal. I told her that she is under no circumstances to be running the roads,"

"Yes sir. We will make sure of that."

As Charlie hung up with David, he turned to Jeremy who was just riding up to him.

"Okay, Jeremy. Do you think you might be prepared for the next race by Saturday?"

"I believe we can swing this. What do you think, Fireball?" Fireball's head went up like he would be ready for anything. By the time they returned home, Jenny was hobbling around on the porch with her crutches.

"Don't you think you should be staying off that foot?" Jeremy asked, being the protective brother as he walked up to the porch.

"Now you are fussing at me? Mom's already fussed at me," she said plopping down on the swing with a small ouch in her face.

"Yes, I am. And you need to stay off that foot as much as possible."

"Yes Dr. Jeremy," she said sighing.

"Don't look at me," Charlie said when Jeremy glanced over at him, "She's your sister." Rosa came out the front door just a fussing in Spanish, and brought out a stool for Jenny to put her foot up on.

"Uh oh," Charlie said "You are in trouble now when she is fussing in Spanish.

"I know," Jenny said raising her foot to rest on the stool, "The bad thing is I understand every word she's saying." Rosa looked up at her surprised, "Would you like me to say in English?"

"Oh no ma'am. I'm telling you they do not want to hear the interpretation. Are you going to follow me around?"

"If I must, I will young lady. You know exactly what the doctor told you, hard head," she said as she gave a knock on her head.

"Rosa, dear. I will help you with dinner," her mom said. It will take the two of us to get miss prissy to follow doctor's orders," she said standing by the door. Rosa was shaking her head. "Well, I'll have to agree with you on that."

Everyone went inside except for Rosa and Jeremy. Jeremy sat down in the rocker next to the swing. "You step the wrong way, you're going to make it worse," he said rocking.

"I know. I think I know when to give in," Jenny said as she looked over at Rosa.

"That is right. You better. I have taken care of you when were sick too. You are going to be upset when your parents go back home at the end of this month,"

"I know," she said with a hand on her tummy, "Well, I'm relieved the baby is okay."

"Amen to that," Rosa said when she raised her foot to put a pillow underneath. Jeremy got up. "Well, I'm going in to help mom in the kitchen." Rosa also went inside. Michael saw and heard everything that was going on and he was standing by the rocker as he tipped it back and forth. It startled Jenny since there wasn't much of a breeze. She looked around.

"Okay," she said out loud. Then Michael sat down in the rocker as he faded into view in front of her and she gasped almost coming up out of the swing.

"It is okay. Calm down Jenny," Michael said waving his hand downward to her.

"Who are you?"

"I am Michael. I am your guardian angel," he said as he noticed her wide eyes and slightly open mouth. "There's a lot weighing on you in taking care of yourself."

"And, and, how do you know?" she asked then simultaneously answered her own question. "Oh, never mind. I guess you would know. What is going on?" she asked almost leaning over.

"Calm down now. Jenny, you should know that you are carrying more than one baby." Her eyes got wider.

"Really??" she questioned getting excited, "I know twins run in mom's family. Is that it?"

"Yes, that's it," Michael said as he gently patted her on her raised leg, "But..."

"Oh great. I do not like the sound of that," she said leaning back with a frown.

"This first trimester is very critical, so you must stay off your feet as much as possible. Your doctor knows what he is talking about."

"Oh wow. He would have said something."

"Jenny, he did not for a reason. It's like that for all the women in your mom's family. With some, they will do okay. But not in your family. You must follow their orders. Your mom would know." Then another frown came across her face.

"Oh," she said solemnly. Michael got up from the rocker. "I knew this time would come eventually that you will see me," and he put his hand gently on her stomach. "Take care of your future." Jenny slightly put her hand over his, "I will. Thank you," she said smiling up at him. Michael smiled, "God will bless you. Do not rush this," then he faded into the scenery around her.

Jenny was sitting still as she still had her hand on her stomach and looked down at her own situation. "Wow. Thank you, God," she said looking up as she heard a voice inside her, "I'll always be with you." She started to cry and wondered "Should I tell him now or later? Her concentration was broken when her mom came out to check on her.

"Sweetheart, are you okay?" Jill asked when she noticed that she was crying.

"Mom, what if I'm having twins?" she asked looking up. Jill eased onto the swing beside her.

"Then you do exactly what I have been telling you. I tell you for a reason baby. I do not want you to lose these babies. Okay?"

"Did that happen with you?" she asked through her tears. Jill took a deep breath, "Yes, it did. It was my second pregnancy and I was so frightened because I did not know of the consequences." Jill put her arm around her daughter and held her for a little as she comforted her.

"I don't want that to happen with you," Jill whispered to her. After ten minutes went by, Jill quietly helped her daughter back inside the house where she sat Jenny down in an arm chair. Jill kissed her on the forehead before returning to the kitchen to check on dinner. Jenny leaned her head back in the arm chair and not realizing how tired she was, fell asleep. It seemed like she had slept a while, when she thought she heard noise coming from the dining room. She rose up onto her crutches and hobbled into the dining room. Looking around the room, it seemed like she was in another era and time. Joseph and his wife were sitting at the table having a serious conversation.

"But honey. How do we keep this from happening? You know my mother has passed away. How would I know?" she asked him with tears in her eyes.

"All I can think of is to ask your cousins and Aunts in the family. Then we take the precautionary measures," Dr. Gordon said, "My dear, in most cases, women can carry on their daily lives without any problems. In this case, I would believe the first trimester is the most crucial and I recommend little to no activity until after that point."

"This is our second pregnancy too," she said leaning back in her chair, "Oh my God, I can only imagine how many in the past generations have lost so many babies!" She begins to weep for the lost ones.

"It is going to be okay, hon. We are going to get passed this and have a beautiful family," Joseph had wrapped his arms around his wife to reassure her.

As Jenny viewed what was happening just before her eyes, she just realized that Joseph was a Family Doctor also. And then she thought she heard someone calling her name from the other room. She went back into the family room.

"I'm here," but no-one was there. As she sat back down in the chair, all she could think about was the many babies who did not make it into the world for so many generations. She closed her eyes praying for others who might have lost their own children. It seemed like no longer than she faded back to sleep she could hear David call her name and gently tapped her on her shoulder.

"Jenny," he said as she gradually opened her eyes," Are you hungry? Dinner is ready."

"Oh yeah. Give me a minute," she said looking up at him.

"You must have had a good nap. You were asleep for a good hour," he said picking up her crutches and giving them to her.

"Yeah. I had a weird dream." He helped her up and they went into the dining room.

During dinner, Jenny was very quiet. When David came over to her afterwards, "You look worried," he whispered to her.

"I am. David, I have a feeling I need to stay in one of the bedrooms downstairs," she said leaning on his shoulder at the table.

"I will stay with you dear. Let's go." He led her into the closest of four bedrooms. Rosa came into the bedroom to freshen it up a little after Jenny had changed into her gown.

"Are you okay dear? You were quiet during dinner."

"I'm a little tired, plus other things are on my mind," Jenny said as Rosa walked into the connecting bathroom. She walked back out with the trash bag in her hand.

"I know you are worried about your bebe's. There is something else I remember from very long time ago. It was shortly after Mrs. Jessie hired me here."

"Oh?" Jenny asked as she sat on the bed, and Rosa came to sit in the bedside chair.

"Si. Mrs. Jessie told me about that Joseph you all were talking about." This aroused her attention.

"I believe it was that he was a Family Doctor early in life. That was when they were trying to conceive a baby."

"What happened?"

"Well, it was not till her third pregnancy when she was able to conceive. And Mrs. Jessie said they were twins. But it took a couple of tries before it happened."

"Oh really?"

"Oh yes, Jenny. That is when it was discovered that any woman in the family who wanted a baby really had to literally stay in bed and no heavy lifting, exercise, or anything until after the first trimester."

"Oh wow. That is about three weeks from now for me,"

Once Jenny settled down, she dozed off to sleep. David called the doctor to confirm what he told Jenny.

"David, it is very important for Jenny not to overdo it until after I see her again. This being her first pregnancy, miscarriages occur quite a bit in a woman's first pregnancy. We need to try to get her past this milestone."

"Ok Doctor Gregory. I will have to keep a closer eye on her."

"And do not let her go up and down those stairs. She can do a little walking. That's all."

"Gotcha. Thank you," David said before he hung up.

The next morning after breakfast, David went over the clinic to see how work was progressing. The foreman, Doug, walked over to chat with him.

"It seems to be going along well. We are already at the half-way point. Once we get this finished, someone can come in and add on the parking lot."

"That's good to know," David said as he surveyed the job site. "So, when do you think the deadline might be?"

"At least three to four weeks, give or take."

"Okay. Thanks Doug. It's going to look nice when its' done. I called the sign company and they will be out in two weeks."

"Good. I just hope it all goes smoothly."

"Yea. Me too."

Afterwards, David went to the track to watch as Jeremy was doing their practice laps. He was relieved that Jill was at the house tending to Jenny. Charlie was on the sideline talking to someone about one of his thoroughbreds. They were discussing the arrangements for the final sale of Jackson.

"Yes, I believe he will enjoy being around the other horses I have. And he has good horsemanship." The man looked around to notice when Jeremy came riding up on Fireball towards Charlie. "It looks like this fine horse is definitely well trained," he said when Fireball slightly rubbed his nose against Charlie's shoulder.

"Yes, he is. We have worked with him for a long time. And Jeremy has been training him and working with him also.," he said smiling over his shoulder at Fireball, "And he's quite the character too."

"How so? Is this one like a playful child?"

"Oh yeah. You can say that," Jeremy said patting the side of Fireball's neck, "He's three and a half years old, and every bit of it."

"I see," the man said smiling. "I have one about the same age. I know exactly what that is like. My Shelly loves to play tricks on me sometimes. And I wonder where in the world she comes up with this stuff." When Fireball heard this, his ears perked up.

"I believe it is just born in them at first. That is, until they get older," Charlie said, "He's a little older and a little bit more disciplined."

"Do you have problems disciplining this one?"

"Fireball? It just might take a little longer with him," Jeremy said, "He'll get there." Fireball looked around at him.

"What's the matter? Do you want to go play now?"

"It seems that he definitely wants a play date," the man said laughing. "I'll bet Shelly would enjoy that. But I'm sure you might want to wait until after the race this Saturday."

"You've got that right," Jeremy said, "We try to keep him focused on that."

"That is a hard job at his age. And I am sure that he will run a great race. He has got spunk," he said shaking Charlie's hand. "I'll see you at the end of the week."

"That sounds good, Mr. Brooks. Is Saturday afternoon okay with you?"

Mr. Brooks nodded and bid them a good day.

"Fireball, I can't believe you did that," Alex said, "I'm wondering how long we'll be able to keep him on his toes now."

"Believe me," Jeremy said, "It'll be something for him to look forward to." Fireball had his head held high like "You've got my attention."

"Fireball, you did make quite an impression on Mr. Brooks," Charlie said. He noticed that David was quiet. "How's Jenny feeling this morning?"

"Oh, she is getting along slowly. We talked this morning before I left. She knows what needs to be done to get past this obstacle. And as you know, it is going to be a little hard for her since she loves to do things. But Rosa will also be there for her. Mama Jill and Roger went to the Sign Shop this morning."

"Awesome," Charlie said, "I do hope she'll make it through this."

"Me too," David said as he sighed.

The next few days were quite busy for most everyone. When David received the date from the Construction foreman the building would be finished, he passed it on to Jenny. Jenny was more than happy to do a write up for the local newspaper for a "Grand Opening" of 'New Horizons.' She was very anxious about this since it would be hopefully be after she sees the doctor again . It was Friday evening when everyone had gathered in the family room.

"Doug said the building will be finished in two weeks from now," David said.

"Okay. And I started writing the notice for the newspaper," Jenny said. Rosa was close by Jenny. "If you go to the race in the morning, I would bring a lawn chair." When Rosa said this, Jenny looked up at David. "That should be okay to do. Right?" she was asking David and her mom.

"I don't see why not," Jill said "We can do that." This seemed to brighten Jenny's day. Rosa was giving one of her grim looks at Jenny, but she ignored it.

They arrived a little early at the track so there wouldn't be any problem in setting the chairs there at the bottom of the seating area on the ground. Sometimes the owners of the horses also set up chairs down below on the grounds.

There was quite a big crowd that showed up for the big race that day. As Jenny was still on her crutches, she was satisfied to be able to be there for Jeremy and Fireball. Jenny watched as the people were walking past them into the stands. Mrs. Doris came walking up and saw Jenny.

"Hey Jenny, do are you doing?" she asked when she gave her a hug.

"I'm hanging in there," Jenny said, "I've got a couple more weeks before I go back to see the doctor."

"Oh, that's good, sweetie. I will be praying for you," Mrs. Doris said patting her hand on her shoulder, "You take good care of yourself. Okay?"

"Oh yes ma'am. Thank you."

David had come and sat down beside her with her parents. She was pleased to be where she was sitting because she saw some of her other friends who lived in town. They all stopped by to say 'Hi' to her on their way into the stands.

As the race was about to begin, David had already fetched a couple of drinks for Jenny and himself. The buzzer went off, and they were off flying down the track. Jeremy was about half way when he started nudging Fireball a little closer to the front of the pack. He felt a little off when he was approaching the final curve going around the race track. Then he realized that the horse next to them was a little too close for comfort, then both went flying into the dirt along with their horses. The others were able to steer around them and keep going towards the finish line.

David and Charlie jumped up out of their seats and ran over to where Jeremy and Fireball had landed in the dirt. "Ouch, what a fall," Jeremy was saying when they made it over to him. Then Jeremy looked over at Fireball to see if he was okay. At first, he was not moving. Charlie came up beside Fireball to check on him.

"Hey boy. Are you okay?" Charlie asked as he noticed that Fireball was able to move his legs around. That was a good sign, but it still concerned Charlie. Fireball gradually got up, as did his partner also. David was helping Jeremy up when he noticed that he was limping.

"I think it's just a small sprain in my knee," Jeremy said as he noticed Alex coming over to help. Jeremy started limping a little bit over to Fireball to check on his buddy. As he walked up to Fireball, with Charlie standing by him; the only thing he could think of doing was wrapping his arms around the horses' neck for a big hug. And Fireball leaned into this special hug, knowing 'Yeah, we're going to be alright We'll get through this together.'

"Hey boy," he whispered in his ear, "You okay? Besides a few bruises?" Fireball gave a soft nudge against him. "Don't worry little dude" Fireball whispered. "Let's not rush it. We have got a whole lifetime together. Right?" 'That is right," Jeremy whispered and backed up to lean on Charlie.

"That was close," Alex said walking over them" Are you okay?" when he saw Jeremy give Fireball a hug.

"Yea I'm okay," Jeremy said wiping tears from his face. "We're going to be okay."

"You know. You will figure out how to quickly move away from others getting in your space. It looks like the other guy is okay. But you might be a little bruised up." Jeremy was standing still for a few minutes while he was getting his bearings. Jenny was watching from the side trying not to jump up and run out to him. They gradually made it over to the side as the race had already finished with another horse call Firewalker who won the race.

Jenny and her parents got up as they came over to them. Alex filled them in.

"They are going to be okay. Jeremy sprained his knee a little, I think Fireball might also need a little extra rest and attention too. Both took a hard fall there."

"Jeremy, can you walk with your knee like that?" Jenny asked.

"Enough to get around. At least it is not broken," he said as she hobbled over to give him a hug.

"Thank God," Jenny said, "That's a last think you need."

"Yeah, well then, we would both be hobbling around the house getting fussed at by Rosa.

"And mom too," Jenny said as she noticed the concerned look on her mom's face. Roger was not too worried because he knew Jeremy was able to bounce back from almost anything.

"I'll be here as long as you both need me," Jill said coming up beside them and she put her arm around Jeremy. "Son, I know you will bounce back in no time. Just promise to take it slow at first. Okay?"

"Yes ma'am. I feel like you are catching up wanting to take care of me from the years missed out on."

"Why of course. I can do that. I hope you don't mind."

"Oh no. I'm not complaining at all," he said as they slowly began to walk down to the stalls. The reporter that was there also came over to Jeremy and Alex.

"You okay man? How is the knee?"

"It is sprained some. But it is nothing that won't heal over time. I think Fireball will be sore for a while."

"Thank you for your time. You take care of that knee," the reporter said before letting them continue down to the horse trailer where David had it parked in front of the stall.

Not long after making it back home, Fireball was fed and he decided he wanted to lie down in his stall and took it easy for the rest of the day. As for Jeremy, Rosa went straight to her medicine cabinet for a good pain killer and a knee wrap she kept around. She fussed over Jeremy long enough to get him to get himself into bed and rest a little. But after she done this, she confirmed with the doctor that she had done the right thing for the situation. Rosa already had knowledge of first aid in the event of situations that just might arise within the time that she had been living and working with the Gordon family.

An hour later, the vet came over to check on Fireball to make sure that he was okay. He got an overall physical and he turned out to be okay. Charlie was relieved that the next race would be about a month later. It would give everyone time to heal and get better. After the vet left, Charlie had gone inside for a little bit. He knew that Mr. Brooks would be coming over later in the day. Joseph popped in to check in on Fireball.

"Hey there boy. How are you doing?" he asked as he rubbed his nose. Fireball kind of shook his head, because although the vet gave him an okay on his health, he was sore. He was starting to get used to Joseph coming around to see him. "I see what you mean. You are sore. Right?" Fireball nodded his head again and looked like he was ready to lie down again. "You go ahead and rest, my boy. It will help you get your strength back." Fireball did not argue, and slowly made his way down for a nap. Soon as he was lying down, Joseph left to check into Jeremy's bedroom. As he faded in by the window, Jeremy was already lying down with his knee propped up on two pillows and snoring. The pain reliever Rosa gave him knocked him out fast which is what he needed. Rosa cared for all of them when any one of them were ever down sick or hurt. She felt like she had pretty much stepped in and done what Mrs. Jessie would have wanted her to do, since she also felt like a step mom. Joseph sat down in the chair for a few minutes to watch over Jeremy. However, he noticed that there was a note pad on the table, and picked it up and read what was written on it. It was the scripture that Jeremy had looked up in the bible a while back. Joseph read through it, and began to ponder what was written there. Then he turned the page over and scribbled something on the back of the page and tore it off. He put the page on the pillow opposite of where Jeremy was laying and left the room.

Meanwhile, downstairs, Jenny was resting in the big armchair that Jeremy usually likes to sit in. Jeremy always enjoyed the comfort of this big chair. In a way, Jeremy thought of it as the warmth of being in the arms of his mom. Jenny would sometimes sit in this chair when he was not there to rest since it was sturdy, yet soft, and she was lying across the chair with her feet hanging down on the other side and snuggled into the corner of the opposite side with a pillow. Charlie and David were outside with Jill and Roger deciding on what was coming up next for the building permits, inspection, and everything else that was needed. Michael was present in the Family room when he noticed that Jenny was asleep in the big arm chair there by the fireplace. She was almost curled up in the middle of the chair and the ceiling fan was on at a medium speed. Michael turned the fan on low; then he picked up the Afghan blanket that was lying across the back of the couch, and he draped it over Jenny. It seemed like she automatically caught it and rolled over into the back of the chair.

"Rest my child. You will need it," he said when he touched her forehead lightly before leaving the room.

"What time is Mr. Brooks coming over?" David asked Charlie as they were walking around the back yard by the swing where Jill and Roger were sitting.

"I talked to him a while ago. He can come by later this afternoon. I know Fireball will want to visit with Shelly."

"That's good. I just walked from the barn, and he is cutting some zz's right now. Rosa finally was able to get Jeremy to go get off his feet, and my dear Jenny is knocked out like she is supposed to when she gets tired out. I told her she does not need to be doing any more than she has to."

"And you didn't have any problem with that?" Jill asked, "I remember when she was younger, getting her to take a nap was like pulling teeth."

"No ma'am. She was tired any way."

"I do hope that she'll be okay," Roger said.

"Yeah, me too. I'm a little worried about this first pregnancy. Getting her to slow down to second gear is hard," David said.

"I know exactly what you mean," Jill said.

By five o'clock, Jeremy was coming to and noticed the note on the pillow beside him. He picked it up and read "I know your deeds, your love and faith, your service and perseverance, and that you are now doing more than you did at first…Rev. 2:19 Keep it up my boy."

When he read the last part of it, he knew it was from Joseph and that he was there. He smiled at that and finally realized that he was doing something right for a change. He just needed to learn how to keep his distance when riding in the races. But his knee wasn't letting him move too fast, so he gradually inched his way to the side of the bed and sat up. Someone was knocking at his door.

"Yea, I'm up. Come on in."

David opened the door and came in. "Hey are you stiff?" David asked as Jeremy nodded yes.

"I would not take it too fast. You must walk first before you began to run. Remember?"

"Oh, believe me, I remember," Jeremy said as he gradually stood up, "Remind me again why I came upstairs."

"You insisted. Surely your memory is not going. Is it?"

"No, I just forgot to pick up that cane Rosa gave me. "

"Okay Jeremy. I will help you downstairs. Just let me know if you are going to use a bedroom downstairs or the couch. It would be advisable at least for a couple of days," David said putting his arm around him.

Jeremy did not feel like fussing with him on this issue because he knew he was right. Once they got down the stairs, Jeremy discovered Jenny still asleep in the arm chair.

"How long has she been asleep?"

"Not too long after you drifted off. I better wake her so she will sleep tonight," David said as Jeremy plopped down on the couch. David slightly shook her shoulder.

"Huh?" she said groggily, opening her eyes.

"Are you going to sleep all night?"

"I could. But I guess I better stay up for a while," she said when she realized the Afghan covering her. "Thanks for the cover."

"I didn't put that over you though," he said and she gave him a funny look and realized who it might have been.

An hour later, Mr. Brooks came by with Shelly in his horse trailer and to pick up Jackson that he had purchased from Charlie. Charlie was just opening the barn door when he was pulling in to see if Fireball was up. He was already up and around. He was looking over his stall to see if she was there yet, then started slowly walking back and forth like he was saying "Let me out, I want to visit a little." Mr. Brooks led Shelly into the barn. She was a beautiful white horse with a flowing mane. Fireball was surprised to see what a beauty she was that he was getting anxious for Charlie to open his gate. Once the barn door was closed and his gate open, Fireball walked out into the middle of the barn, proud to be a horse. By his demeanor, you can tell how excited he was to finally meet Shelly. And yet he remembered how sore he was, so he decided to take it slow. He walked up to Shelly and they met face to face as if they were giving each other a once over inspection. If you could understand their language, they did a small neigh and a nicker. A nicker was a sign of 'Hi, how are you.' It is like a greeting sound among horses. And the neigh is saying 'I see you.' They both stood there for a few minutes in their own little conversation as the others snuck out the barn door and headed toward the house.

"I do believe Fireball has a liking for Shelly," Charlie said smiling.

"I agree with you on that," Mr. Brooks said as they strolled toward the porch. Rosa had coffee waiting for them in the family room and they had a chance to sit and visit for a while.

Mr. Brooks was impressed with the manners that Fireball did have around Shelly.

"Oh, don't be deceived, Mr. Brooks," Charlie said, "He enjoys being around other horses and running through the meadow care free every chance he gets."

"So, he's a free spirit also?"

"Yes, he is indeed. I know one thing for sure. If I let him loose for a while, I believe he would have fun running through the meadow behind the house and checking out the beach. And after he would get tired, he would return home ready for dinner."

They both laughed at the thought. "And I do believe that Shelly would be right beside him doing the exact same thing."

Later Jenny and David made it out to the corral to see the horses enjoying their visit.

"Wow. She is beautiful," Jenny said as David put his arm around her.

"Yeah, she is. I can see why Fireball perked up this afternoon. I thought he was sore?"

"Me too. I guess he forgot all about that for now."

"Could very well be," she said as they watched the two horses for a little bit before they realized that Shelly had slowly made her way over to where they were standing by the fence. Fireball had followed behind and came up beside her. Shelly had sensed something in Jenny. Jenny was surprised that she had come straight over to her. She looked up at David in awe smiling and she reached out and stroked Shelly's nose. Shelly came a little closer towards Jenny and in a slight slow movement eased her head beside Jenny's head like a hug. And the next most unusual thing that happened was that Shelly moved back and put her nose down toward Jenny's belly.

Jenny looked down and then back up and she came face to face with her again.

"You know I have got a baby inside. Don't you?" All Shelly could do that was so gentle in a way; she nudged her hand with her nose.

"Wow!"

"That could either be a good or bad sign," Alex said when he noticed what happened from his truck and was walking over to them.

"How do you mean?" Jenny asked.

"Horses can sense more than you think, Jenny. If I were you, I would ask the doctor earlier than you want."

"I do not understand. Do they sense when something is wrong?"

"Uh huh, they sure can," Alex said nodding his head, "Most animals of creation can sense things like that not to mention when trouble's coming or when a storm's brewing and they take cover." She looked at him. Alex was very serious about that. And he seemed genuinely concerned for Jenny and her pregnancy. She looked down at her tummy and back over at Shelly and Fireball even gave her the same look as did Shelly.

"Wow! I didn't know that."

"Horses can sense when a woman is pregnant by the smell of your body chemistry. Chances are Fireball already knows. You have seen how different he is when he's around you," Alex said.

"That's interesting to know," David said as Jenny agreed with him. Jenny knew that the doctor's office would have been closed by now, so she decided to wait and call him in the morning and try to go in to see him. Not long after that, Mr. Brooks came out with Charlie to load Jackson into the horse trailer.

"Looks like they're enjoying this little play date," Mr. Brooks said, "She's not going to want to go home just yet." He made a clicking noise that got her attention and she pranced over to him by the fence and looked back over at Fireball.

"I know girl. Just a little longer?" She responded with one ear cocked back as she looked at him and back over at Fireball, "Alright girl. Just a little longer."

The following morning, Jenny was able to make an appointment to see Dr. Gregory at mid-morning. When he came into the room, Jenny was sitting on the exam table with the gown on as requested where the sonogram equipment was located. David and Jill were in the room with her.

"You look a little worried, Jenny," he said as she nodded. And then she lay down on the table. "Okay," he said putting some lubricant on her belly, "Let's see what is going on here. You haven't overdone things, have you?"

"No sir. I don't think so. I have done as you requested. It's hard since I'm an active person." Once he started rolling the instrument over her belly, he was looking to see if everything was where they should be. He did notice that there were two inside and he swapped places with the nurse and put his stethoscope on to listen for the heartbeats. After a few minutes of "oh and uh huh," Dr. Gregory looked at the screen and back up at Jenny.

"What's wrong?" Jenny asked concerned, as David and Jill were also curious. Then he put the stethoscope on Jenny to listen to it.

"Listen. How many heartbeats do you hear?"

Her face went solemn, "One."

"Yep, I was afraid of that," he said as he saw the expressions on their faces, "However Jenny, the good part is that you just made it to your first trimester."

"What do you think we should do? Is there something that can be done?"

"The other good part is that you still have a baby that is alive! I feel better if you go ahead and go through your full cycle before we do anything else. I do not want to take any extra risks with your baby that's now still alive inside of your womb. It is going to feel strange for a while but you will get through it. There's one thing I believe strongly in that I hope that you're doing."

"What's that?"

"Listen to upbeat music. Whatever kind of music you like to listen to, be it soft rock, classical or Christian music. This will help you keep going physically, emotionally, and it will also enhance the growth and nurture of your baby. The more it feels the love inside of you taking care of yourself, and the things you do for your child; he will thrive and grow stronger while inside of your womb. Okay?"

"Okay," she said with a smile, "That I can and will do, Anything else?"

"Yes, stay away from the stairs for now. You will get your shape back in no time the way you work out. So, a little bit of exercise won't hurt; and please make sure to eat a healthy diet. This little one will need it," he said with a smile on his face and he put his hand on her belly, "You can do this Jenny. Believe in yourself. Okay?"

"Okay. I think I have got that down pretty good."

"Well, when you took that fall down the stairs, I tend to think that just maybe you had too much on your plate at the time, and you were worried about a lot of things. Stop worrying. Look how many family members you have around you. That is what they are here for."

"That's right Jenny," Jill spoke up, "I'm still trying to get her to slow down some more," And the doctor kind of grinned at that.

"I propose that you do what you must do for the health of this little one. God did bless you still with a baby inside of you that wants to live."

"Yes, he did," she whispered, "Like you said, it's going to feel a little strange, but I believe I can do this," Jill and David were relieved that only one was spared. And Jenny left the doctor's office in better spirits.

It was almost noon when Charlie came into the family room where Jeremy and Jenny were lounging in their chairs.

"Hey guys. I have got something you might want to read in the newspaper," he said sitting on the couch.

"Oh? What is that?" Jeremy asked as Charlie handed him the Sports section. There was a picture of when he had given Fireball a hug. The title was 'Now That's Devotion!" It read, "The photograph was taken as owner and rider, Jeremy Smythe Brooks, limped over to his horse, Fireball for an inspiring hug. This just goes to prove that horses have feelings too. You could see the strong connection of these two as they comforted each other. Even though yes, we come to cheer for our favorite horse to win, there is usually in every rider with their horse, a close companionship that grows and thrives as they work and train together week after week for a chance in a lifetime to win in the races. However, this just goes to prove that there is more in life than just winning. It is the friendship and comradery between all these folks. We believe in you, Jeremy, and Fireball. We know that you will make a comeback and prove to your ancestors that 'Yes, you can do this and you're as good as your ancestors before you.' You both have the determination and spirit."

After reading this Jeremy was awestruck "Wow! That is so cool. I did not even know he took a picture," He passed it over to Jenny to let her read it. By the time she finished reading it, there were tears rolling down her cheeks, "That is so beautiful," she said smiling through her tears, "That's a first time I've read anything like that."

Jeremy got up and went out to the stable with his cane and paper in tow. As he approached the barn door, he noticed that Fireball was standing up in his stall.

"Hey Fireball," I've got something that will really lift your spirits," he said walking over and he looked up from chewing on a carrot.

"Oh really? What 'cha got there?"

Jeremy read the short article to him after showing him the picture that was taken of them.

"Whoa. We did not win the race. What a touching story they wrote," he said. Jeremy reached over the gate and rubbed him lightly on his neck.

"Yeah. That means they are looking forward to seeing us back on the track."

"Right. After we get to feeling better," Fireball replied, "Are there any more carrots? I am hungry. And before you ask, I did have my regular food."

"No problem," he said reaching for a bag of carrots hanging on the post nearby, "Here you go," as he passed him a couple of carrots, "This will help you heal and feel better. You need to get your strength back."

After chewing on the carrot, Fireball said "If I knew it was hanging that close, I would've already grabbed it myself." Jeremy kind of laughed at him.

"Boy, you're something else." Jeremy said. He stayed with Fireball for a little while before returning to the house.

There was a small breeze coming through the barn as birds flew in. A song bird landed there on the rail as Fireball finished eating the last carrot. He looked over at the bird, as he perched there in between his and Chantilly's stall. The bird walked around then stopped in one spot and started to sing a beautiful song for them. Before he knew it, Fireball was falling asleep again.

A couple of days went by. At the job side, construction was under way as usual and going well. Doug, the foreman noticed that they were ahead of schedule as they were getting closer to the end of their project. He called David and told him the good news that they will be finished in two weeks. The sign 'New Horizons' was also going up that same day.

Jenny went into the kitchen to grab an apple out of the fruit basket on the counter. Jenny knew that her mom had already told Rosa about what happened at the doctor's office. Rosa was picking up dishes from the dishwasher as she came in, so she pulled out the orange juice to pour Jenny a glass.

"Rosa, you do not have to fuss over me, you know. The good news is we still have a baby to bring into the world. And I am going to do the best I can to make it stronger."

"You have to make yourself stronger also, my child," Rosa said as she had wrapped her arms around her, "I'll make sure that you get all the nutrients you need."

"I know you will Rosa. Thank you for looking after us and everything you do. I do appreciate that in you."

"Yes, child. I do. I feel like the stepmother now. You know, the good stepmother."

"Yes, you are. And you are doing a great job."

"Okay," Rosa said wiping her hands on her apron, "I will always want to care for you when you need it, young lady."

"I'm going to go sit outside on the swing for a while," Jenny said turning around on her crutches, "Have you heard from my regular doctor when I get to come out of this cast?"

"No dear. But I will call for you and find out. I will let you know." Rosa assisted her in making her way outside and propped her foot on the foot stool once she got comfortable. Rosa went back inside to call the doctor's office and begin preparing something for lunch. Jill met Rosa back in the kitchen.

"Rosa, dear. We have decided."

"Yes ma'am?"

"Roger and I decided to stay a little longer than we planned. We just want to make sure Jenny and Jeremy's going to be okay. I hope that you don't mind."

"Oh no ma'am. It is quite enjoyable having you around to visit with and talk to especially when you know Mrs. Jenny can be stubborn and going from one thing to the next. You know how she is. Unpredictable."

"Oh yes. She likes to be spontaneous. After having this baby, I believe she just might try to slow down a little bit."

"Oh, I do hope you are right. I never know what is coming up next. But they do try to keep me posted. And there's days when Jeremy just loves his pizza; Charlie likes hamburgers, David, and Chinese food? Then there's Jenny. She throws a whammy occasionally. Do you remember that day she was having a craving for Shrimp and what was it?"

"Lobster. That is what it was," Jill said. "I can see how hard it could be to keep any kind of balanced diet going on around here. I tell you what Rosa," Jill said sitting down at the bar," We're going to come up with some new ideas that you can throw in once in a while to help keep them on track."

"Ooh. I like your thinking, Mrs. Jill." Then the two began to put their ideas together and down on paper. Rosa was ready for some new menu ideas to keep crew happy.

Jenny was at a slow swing as she watched Fireball out in the corral and thought about what had happened the other day. "Shelly, my girl," she thought out loud, "I might just see if you are up for sale, or if Mr. Brooks might consider it. I would like to bring you to Fireball."

She could not help but think about the stillborn inside of her womb also. But if it meant the safety and wellbeing of her other baby's survival, she was going to do the best she could. And she began to play some of the music that she enjoyed listening to. She got a crazy notion in her head as she sat there wondering about it, then she called Anne, the nurse at Dr. Gregory's office. She got an answer that was very doable. "Yes! Thank you," she said to the nurse. She was not about to go hunting David down, so she called him on her cell phone

"Yes dear. Where are you? Upstairs? What are you doing? Awe. Can you come downstairs?'

"I've got a great idea we can do together."

Once he came outside, "What is up? Or should I ask what you got up your sleeve?"

"I asked the nurse first. Okay? And I really want to see if Fireball will let me ride him."

"Are you serious?" he asked giving her a crazy look.

"Why yes, I am serious. And the nurse said its okay. She did ask the doctor also," she said enthusiastically.

"Ok dear. Let's go then. You worry me sometimes." He helped her up on her crutches and down the porch steps. Once they made it into the barn, Jenny hobbled over to Fireball who was coming in from the corral.

"Fireball," Jenny said, and stopped two feet from her. "Will you let me ride you for a little bit?" It looked like he was thinking for a minute; but then he bowed his legs down as a 'Welcome' sign. She looked at David. "Has Jeremy been training him to do this?"

"Not that I know of. Of course, with them two, you never know. I do believe that is a good sign. Right?"

"Yeah, I think so," she said as he went to pull down Fireball's blue blanket from the hook on the wall, and laid on top first before he proceeded to set the saddle on his back. After that, David also saddled up Chantilly for him to ride. Then it took a few minutes to help Jenny get up on Fireball before he got up on Chantilly. Just as they were about to come out of the barn, here comes Jeremy hobbling a three-legged walk with his cane. But he was getting around pretty good.

"Who said you could ride horses?" Jeremy asked.

"I'll have you know that I called the doctor first before I even thought about doing this."

"Oh really? Fireball, and you let her? Fireball nudged him on his shoulder as if he was reassuring Jeremy that it was okay. "Okay, you be careful with her now," Jeremy said backing up to let them by.

"Thank you. Did you get that from dad? You sure do sound just like him."

"Probably so," he said, "Please be careful sis." He had tended to let his nurturing side show lately more around his sister as they have begun to grow closer as brother and sister. He did not realize it until lately.

"Wow. Did I just say that?" he asked himself after they had already passed by. "I must be tripping."

"No, you're just maturing Jeremy," he heard the familiar voice of Michael. He almost lost his balance.

"Michael? What a coincidence. I was just thinking about you."

"Same here. How are you feeling? Are the limbs starting to loosen up a little?" Michael asked with concern in his voice.

"I am getting there. I figured that I better start doing some walking around today. I get out here and Jenny is on the horse. I am not so sure that's a brilliant idea."

"But it is also therapeutic for her and for Fireball, don't you think? How does it make you feel after a short little ride like that?"

"Oh. Yeah, you are right. I guess in a way that will also help Fireball get used to her being pregnant. Right? And he is already aware of what's going on."

"That's right Jeremy. Stranger things have happened. Well, don't let that knee get you down too much."

"I won't. I've got other things to think about. Once we get back in the saddle, my partner and I need to concentrate on dodging those other riders. That's one thing I don't want to happen again," Jeremy said leaning on his cane.

"There you go. That is the spirit. I saw the renovations of the building. Looks like it's coming along great."

"Oh good. David told us that it will be coming to completion soon. I am so looking forward to that."

"Jeremy, you have grown so much this year. You have matured a lot and grown spiritually also," Michael said, "I can see that you have discovered the greatest values in life. And that is important for you to be able to grow in all of your relationships," Michael said reaching out his hand to Jeremy. Then Michael was astonished when Jeremy had voluntarily reached out and hugged him.

"Thank you, Michael, for being here for me and Jenny. You don't know how much I really did need your guidance."

"Oh, believe me. Yes, I do know. This is my purpose here on earth. But even when I'm not here, God's spirit will always be with you to guide you."

"Is this good-bye for now?"

"Yes, it is Jeremy. I do have a few projects that I was given to do. But I will be seeing you in the future. You take good care of yourself and your sister," Michael said before he gave Jeremy another hug.

"I do appreciate it." Then Michael started walking down the middle of the barn and faded into the scenery around him.

"I'll miss you Michael," Jeremy said. He stood there for a few minutes before he turned around and began walking toward the back yard to sit in the swing and watch his sister riding Fireball.

As they walked slowly around the meadow, Fireball was so gentle with her. Chantilly looked around at him ad if she was talking to him. Only Fireball knew what his mom was saying to him when he noticed her glancing back at him. David took it slow with Chantilly. As for Chantilly, she was the gentlest horse they ever had, and did not intend to let her leave the family.

Within the next two weeks after Jenny had talked to Dr. Gregory, he told her that it would increase her mentality if she wanted to ride Fireball once a day, so long as they took it slow. When David heard this, he seemed satisfied with the answer. So, he did go with her around the same time every day for a short ride while Jeremy was also getting better and gradually got away from the cane. During this week, Jill and Roger started working on the room that Jenny chose as the baby's room. Jenny had decided to keep using the bedroom downstairs and use the bedroom that was connected to theirs for the baby's room. Jenny looked over a catalog that Jill brought home for them to look through for the different items and furniture she wanted to put in there. Jenny was pleased that her parents were able to stay longer to help them out a little. By the end of the week, Jenny was able to get out of the foot cast; but was told to also go slow in her walking around without the crutches.

A few times this week, David noticed her sitting in the rocking chair in the family room with her head phones on and listening to music from her cell phone. A couple of days after the final renovations of 'New Horizons' were finished; Jenny was sitting in the rocking chair when Jeremy came in and sat down beside her.

"Hey. Let's put on some music on the entertainment center."

"Okay. Sounds good to me." He walked to a small shelf of CDs where he chose a few different ones he knew that she always enjoyed listening to. When he put on a Christian contemporary cd of Randy Travis, she looked up at him.

"How'd you know I was thinking of that one?"

"Oh, he's one of my favorites too," he said when he came over and sat down beside her. The music filled the house as they also had a few small speakers that were scattered around the house. Then everyone started coming in from different directions of the house and made themselves comfortable . Even Alex followed Charlie in from the kitchen where they sneaking a couple of oatmeal cookies that Rosa had just got out from the oven. Rosa had returned to the kitchen and thought she would catch them red-handed. But decided that did not matter. She went ahead and dished them onto a serving tray and brought them into the family room and she set them down on the coffee table. Roger and Jill came downstairs from their room to sit in on the family gathering. Jenny was finally in a good mental state with her baby growing inside of her now, After the Randy Travis cd was finished. David picked one that he knew everyone liked. Once he put it on, everyone knew that it was the Oakridge Boys. It was one that all enjoyed the different songs that they did young and old, the songs touched each one as they listened to the music. Jenny looked down to see a piece of paper close to the rocker that she had not noticed before. Once she read it, she passed it around for everyone to read.

"But as for you, be strong and do not give up, for your work will be rewarded – 2 Chronicles 15:7. For great is his love toward us, and the faithfulness of the Lord endures forever. Praise the Lord. – Psalm 117:2. I leave you now my family. Be strong and prosper in the Lord. Lean on each other for your support and

encouragement. As for you, my brothers, and sisters in Christ, lean not on your own understanding; but stand firm in your Faith; and you will all grow within the Love and Grace of our Lord Jesus Christ. My peace, I leave you. May He always Bless you in all that you do. — Your third cousin, Joseph Ralph Gordon.

EPILOGUE

It was two weeks later, both Jeremy and Jenny were back on their feet and more stable. Jenny was walking better without the crutches and her ankle had healed. As for Jeremy, the only exercise he could do until he was strong enough was walking. But it kept him going along with Fireball who would also go walking with him in the meadow. They were out in the back, walking around the meadow together. Sometimes Fireball would wander a little further, take a lap around the meadow, and catch back up with him. Fireball was a free-spirited horse, who enjoyed the freedom of wandering around in the meadow with Jeremy as much as racing. But he was patiently waiting for his partner to heal completely before they could enter the next race. "You are enjoying this. Aren't you?" Jeremy asked him. And Fireball's ears were relaxed to the sides like he was thinking "Yes, this is relaxing and I'm walking with you." Then for a moment, he stopped and raised his head like something got his attention. Fireball heard a familiar truck pulling into the driveway up front. He looked back at Jeremy.

"Do you want me to get on?" Jeremy asked. Fireball stood still for him to climb into the saddle. No sooner than Jeremy got a hold of the reins, Fireball took off. Jeremy knew what he was excited about, so he hung on as they rode up to the barn where Mr. Brooks was driving up with the horse trailer in tow and parked. Once Fireball slowed down to a stop, Jeremy got down.

"Looks like you two are doing much better," Mr. Brooks said he shook Jeremy's hand.

"Yes sir. Sure 'nuff. It's good to see you." He went around to open the trailer and Fireball was following right behind him. Once the door was opened, Shelly comes prancing out into the open. The rest of the family came out from the house to see her arrival.

"Happy Birthday Fireball," Jeremy said when Fireball gave him a funny look, "Really?"

"Fireball," Mr. Brooks said "Shelly is now all yours." Fireball looked at him and then back to Jeremy; but he wasted no time in approaching Shelly as he came over to her neck to neck in a hug. Everyone smiled at this. Once they came out of their hug, Fireball walked over to Mr. Brooks and put his head on his shoulder as if he was saying to him 'Thank you.'

"You're most welcome my boy." Then Shelly had also walked over to Jeremy and had done the same thing. That day Fireball and Shelly enjoyed a birthday party that started out their new bond together. It was a joyous occasion for the Gordon family to bring a little extra something special into the life of Fireball.

Monday morning, there was a crowd of people there in the parking lot of 'New Horizons.' And the local Television station crew were also present to mark this event. The spokeswoman, Mrs. Doris Barclay, was holding the microphone.

"Ladies and gentlemen. We are all gathered here today to pay tribute to a great lady of the community, Mrs. Jessie Gordon; and to celebrate a new beginning in life as her family has not only expanded; but we have gone up two more floors to this building that stands before us. It was six years ago, when Mrs. Jessie Gordon began this project as another way of reaching out to our community for medical needs within the family. That was when she approached my husband, Reverend Harold Barclay, and myself about being a part of this ministry that we all had in common. The work of the Lord is a common area where families come together as one to fill the needs of others and make their lives more enriching, as we work together all for the common good. I believe that I can speak for Mrs. Jessie, when I say 'Thank you' to everyone in her family for all their hard work, dedication, devotion and love they put into everything they do together as a team, as a family. I have seen them go through a few changes lately, and not to mention, a new addition to the family that I understand will be born in October of this year.

David looked over at his glowing wife, Jenny, who was four months along now, and she smiled back at him as he held her hand.

"There is something new that I have learned over these past few weeks of the Gordon family. The niece of Mrs. Jessie Gordon, Mrs. Jenny Smythe Bridges, is now the new mistress of the Gordon Villa. She intends to step in and pick up where her Aunt Jessie started; and continue in partnership with her husband, David Bridges; her brother, Jeremy Smythe; and her cousin, Charlie Gordon in their endeavors to finish the race that is set before them. And I know in my heart and see it in their Faith that they are all up for the challenge no matter what comes before them."

www.ingramcontent.com/pod-product-compliance
Lightning Source LLC
LaVergne TN
LVHW012059070526
838200LV00070BA/3257